Beneath London's Fog

Iona Caldwell

FyreSyde
publishing

For information contact :

FyreSyde Publishing

https://www.fyresydepublishing.com

Cover design by Olivia on Fiverr

ISBN: 9780578488899

Paperback Edition

10 9 8 7 6 5 4 3 2 1

I. The Streets Ran With Blood

I want it known before this tale begins – I am not a hero but a villain. I want no sympathy from whomever reads this recalling of my story; no mourning for the tragedy that befell my life. I am not an innocent man but a sinner forced to face the ravaging demons and ghosts of his own creation.

My story began as many do – a lie, a fire and murder. One of my kind murdered the woman I loved in the coldest of blood in one of history's darkest times at the behest of a possessive noble.

After a run in with him in Nottingham, I soon found myself fleeing for my life from hunters, framed for a murder I had not committed.

Forgive me, I am getting ahead of myself.

Let me begin where this part of my story took place.

A bloody civil war ravaged London followed shortly by the Great Fire in 1666. A glorious time for me and those like me to take advantage of the chaos and remain hidden in the shadows.

I managed to pursue the one responsible for nearly getting me killed two centuries prior to the plague which befell London before the fire.

Within the shadows of the flickering flames of St. Peter's Cathedral, I struck him down and departed the city, thus avoiding my demise.

I had yet to escape him, however, when his vengeful spirit devoured the souls of the innocent in a mad bloodlust.

Though greatly injured, I managed to drive his spirit to my new home Raven Hollow Manor in London, imprisoning him in stone coffin in the crypt beneath it.

Peace resumed in my life and nobles of all kinds enjoyed lavishly hosted parties within the halls of my estate.

Unfortunately, the short lived splendor at the hands of the hauntings filled the ears of the locals and my beloved home decayed into a tangled web of blood-filled rumors and superstition.

My once glorious halls became infested with dust, its crystal chandeliers covered with cobwebs, their spiders fat on the insects buzzing around the decay and mold-covered wallpaper.

Yet, there I remained as it proved a decent place to not only contain my greatest sin but served also as a castle of solitude.

The tides of time swept by in a cacophony of modernization and the movement from superstition to things only mortal science could explain.

I still needed to venture into the city, not only to feed but also to purchase other items needed for everyday living.

It wasn't until the winter of 1910 that my silence would be disrupted in the form of a girl named Holly, a young street urchin accused of theft. I took her with me after using a bit of "persuasion" on the local officers to let her go.

They did not need to know where I would take her and she soon grew into a wonderful messenger on my behalf. She became a rather attractive young woman with bouncy blonde curls who kept me company with stories of what went on in the city.

I am sure, at one time, she became infatuated with me. It did not surprise me. To mortals, my kind held a certain allure they found difficult to ignore. I ended her infatuation quickly following a stern talking to and dousing with cold water.

One day, while in my labyrinthine garden, Holly came to me in tears.

When the people of London learned where Holly lived, the townsfolk dubbed her a practitioner of black magic.

One day, I found Holly sitting on one of the marble benches in the garden, sobbing. I picked a flower and put it in my daughter's hair, sitting next to her beneath the statue of a praying angel.

3

"You need not worry about them, dearest. Mortals are always quick to place labels on what they do not understand."

Holly sniffled and sobbed, wiping her nose and offering me a smile. "But why do they avoid this place, Jonathan?"

"Mortals fear what they cannot comprehend. Pay them no mind. You are a wonderful young woman," I purred, brushing a blonde curl from her face.

The words appeared to have placated her as she smiled and joined me in a moonlight stroll through the garden.

* * *

Around midnight, after dinner with Holly, I dismissed her to bed. Once she departed, I sought out sustenance in the city.

A dense fog rolled in due to the cool winter weather and the recent days of rain.

Combined with the darkness of the streets and alleyways, I managed to meet a young working woman on the corner and wooed her into joining me for a walk to the park. As with other women, I made sure she understood I respected her body with gentle caresses and loving words murmured into her ears.

Once I placed her deep under my spell, I kissed the tender flesh of the woman's throat and exposed shoulder, thanking her for her gift.

My fangs pierced her flesh, earning a moan of pleasure as her body surrendered its precious life force without any significant damage. Her body pressed against mine, her moans increasing with pleasure at my kiss.

I preferred this method to those of many of my other brethren who tore their victims apart during a feeding, choosing power to subdue instead of sexual allure.

When signs of weakness began manifesting I released my hold, picking her up after licking the small puncture wounds, my saliva healing them, leaving no marks or scars.

To assure she received care, I took her to the nearest hospital and deposited her on the steps without anyone noticing.

As always, I used hypnotic suggestion to erase her memory and leave her with a pleasant dream.

During the wee hours of the morning, I tended to enjoy the calls of the birds and the chirping of the crickets to help relieve the burden on my mind.

Not a soul roamed the streets near the bridge where I liked to sit and write poetry or read a book.

In the midst of the silence, a horrifying shriek caught my attention, almost startling me.

My pupils narrowed to those one might see in a viper or a cat. I let my body dissipate into the form of a black mist, hovering over the city in search of the source of the scream.

I found it in the shape of the body of a mangled man.

The whites of his eyes consumed most of the portion of the glossy orbs in his skull, mouth gaped open mid-scream.

I knelt before him, my own brows furrowed in frustration at the recognition of the familiar puncture wounds on the man's throat. *This cannot be. No other has hunted here in centuries.*

The disturbing find made something clear.

Many of my kind preferred not to hunt in one place occupied by another of higher status, or in another's territory for that matter. We changed due to the growing number of human hunters who would kill any of us they came across.

Despite the city's size, my reputation often kept others out of my hunting grounds, for which I remained grateful.

This new kill had been malicious.

If I allowed such behavior to continue, it could draw the attention of the hunters or the local police to my home.

Whomever the responsible party, I needed to locate them and have a word with them or kill them if necessary.

My eyes closed, a heavy sigh drawing up from within my lungs. I placed my fingers over the man's eyes, using a gentle touch to close them. "Forgive whichever of us did this to you. You did not deserve to die in such a horrific manner."

Searching through the pockets of his trench coat, I located his identification card and vowed to send some money and roses to his family.

Sounds of sirens and the calls of the corner watchmen announced the arrival of the authorities. I left them the man's wallet so they could inform his family of their loss.

I lurked in the shadows listening to the inspectors scrutinizing the scene.

"Bloody mystery, it is. This is the second mangled body we found this week. One has to wonder if we might be witnessing the birth of another blighter of a serial killer." One of the inspectors scratched his head beneath the dome shaped hat.

I recognized him as Bertrand Abrams, a well-known officer and one of the only men who aided Holly during her visits to town.

From his looks, one would expect him to hail from Scotland. A bushy mustache and stringy hair with the consistency of sheep's wool held the color of fire. Dimples set into high cheekbones and a double chin made me smile. A portly belly betrayed his affinity for too many scones and perhaps Scotch.

He had been wrong. This death held no mystery. I merely needed to find the one responsible before it resulted in too much of a personal dilemma.

Following the release of the corpse to the medical examiner, I took the form of black mist and drifted back to Raven Hollow.

The beginnings of my night would be haunted by dreams of a past filled with love, vengeance and pain.

It would be filled with shining auburn locks and eyes the color of the fresh leaves of spring.

II. Annabelle

London, Summer 1565

I stood in the shadows of the balcony in a room full of people in London's upper class, a glass of champagne in my hand, my eyes following the path of a young woman as she drifted from group to group—her strawberry lips plump and perfect for a summer night's kiss. I fantasized about what it might feel like to taste her lips beneath the moonlight.

At times I caught the woman glancing at me, a shy smile on her face.

Beneath the ornate feline mask, I caught eyes colored with facial shadow, half-lidded with as much desire as I felt welling up within me. The glances and flirting gestures occurred so often through the night I could take no more and approached her.

The woman covered her face with a frilly, cream fan, gesturing her head towards the opened window panes leading to the granite balcony.

The satin curtains danced in the warmth of the breeze, their soft whooshes unheard by the gossiping guests as the woman moved through them.

With immortal grace, I glided through the bodies, refusing advances from bourgeoisie ladies whose breasts struggled to remain hidden behind their laced corsets.

When I reached the young woman, she stood staring out at the lavish gardens below. My eyes never left her face, entranced by her porcelain skin almost shining in the moon's light.

Below, gurgling water echoed from the fountain in the middle of the stone pathway, surrounded by beautiful flowers blooming, permeating the air with sensual smells.

"Greetings, my lady." I took her silken gloved hand and placed a kiss on the back of her knuckles. My hazel eyes locked on her bright green gaze.

We appeared to be studying one another. The sounds of the party faded into nothingness the further we drifted into our own world.

Thoughts of what she might be thinking ran through my mind along with concerns I often held during such encounters. Did she fall victim to my wiles? My natural seduction or did she feel a natural attraction?

A brief sense of ache pushed at the walls of my beating heart. I forced the thoughts away. It could not be. If my seduction did indeed affect her, she would not have teased me as much as she did. Attraction would have been instant as it had been with those other women from the party who shoved their large bosoms in my face as I walked by.

"To you as well, sir," She replied, gesturing a slight nod.

Her bright smile set my heart ablaze with the desire. I gathered my will and requested her to dance with me, an offer she agreed to, never letting go of the mischievous tease of a grin lighting her lips.

I led us to the ballroom where I proceeded to guide her through the most graceful dance. My hand held firm around her tiny waist while her frilly dress followed each majestic spin with the rhythm of the music.

During a dip, I ventured to ask her what her name could be.

The woman giggled, fanning herself and requesting some fresh air in light of so much dancing. I obliged her and guided her back to the balcony.

In the distance, I could hear the bubbling sound of the water cascading in the fountain. All around the smell of flowers drifted in the cool summer breeze. To give her a rest, I helped her sit on one of the marble benches, joining her.

I repeated my request to know her name.

She pushed one of the loosened curls of her bronze hair away from her face. Her green eyes threatening to delve into the depths of my soul. "I am Annabelle Price. May I ask your name], my Lord?"

"Jonathan Holloway. It is my greatest pleasure to make your acquaintance, Ms. Price."

Annabelle giggled. "Annabelle, please. To you as well, Mr. Holloway."

As she had done with me, I corrected her to use my first name.

Little had I known that night would lead to more meetings in the near future only to end in a tragedy which would begin my descent into the darkness of vengeance.

* * *

Light tapping followed by Holly's voice calling out to me through the closed door caused me to groan, rising in bed and calling to her to give me a moment. Immense pressure threatened to tear my eyes from my skull as I lumbered over to the rack in the corner of the room where a black, silk robe hung.

I put on the robe, taking in the tangled sandy mess of shortened hair in the mirror before staggering over to the door, opening it.

As usual, Holly managed to make herself look beyond beautiful despite the early hours of the day. Her bouncy honey-blonde curls sat at the top of her head in a formal bun, her cream dress and green overcoat glistening with the light of the sun. Plump cheeks, colored with a slight hint of blush drew up in a deep-dimpled grin.

"Good morning," She greeted.

Rubbing my eyes, ignoring the annoyance niggling my mind, I returned her greeting. "Holly, you know I am not a morning man. What could you possibly need so early?"

Holly pursed her lips, her blue eyes displaying irritation. "Well, that's rude. I wanted to have breakfast together like we used to. Were you out late again?"

I nodded.

My body ached from fatigue, the muscles heavy and throbbing with want to go back to bed.

When she continued to plead, I sighed and asked her for some time to allow me to get a bath and join her downstairs.

Despite my belief to the contrary, Holly's dimpled grin grew wider, eyes shining with excitement.

It made me regret all of those mornings I sent her away, choosing to sleep until after sunset.

Holly placed a kiss on my cheek, thanking me, prancing off like a deer through a field of grain back down the stairs.

I returned to my room to procure some clothes for myself and mosey into the bathroom where I ran a hot bath, letting the warm water fill the tub and ease my aching body. I added some of the scented oils and foreign bath salts I purchased during one of my rare visits to the bustling London market.

They eased the stress and lingering pain, allowing me to relax into a peaceful state of mind. My head lulled back to stare at the ceiling as I thought about the dream recounting the time I met Annabelle, the woman I loved more than my own life. The woman I watched helplessly murdered with my own eyes.

I remembered the crimson streams of blood, the life leaving her eyes as she reached out to me, gurgling out my name before she fell to the ground.

Never before had I felt such pain. Such loss.

Not now. I cannot allow myself to drift into despair. Not when my daughter waits for me. I rose from the bath, dried myself with one of the soft cotton towels.

I dressed to join Holly in the kitchen, stopping by my dresser to look at a small, ornate box. I opened it to find a necklace and a ring, sighing at the memories they held. Its bronze hinges creaked when I closed the lid and left the room to go downstairs.

Holly sat at the table, standing when she saw me, moving like the wind to prepare me a plate containing a full English breakfast and a cup of tea with cream and sugar.

Holly joined me, her head turned away towards the table, hands twiddling in her lap.

I opened the paper she got me and proceeded to read, ignoring her since I knew the behavior to mean she had something she wished to ask.

I sighed, unable to handle her less than subtle attempts to get my attention. "What is it? I know you have something you wish to say," I asked, lowering the paper.

Biting her lower lip, Holly whimpered. "I wondered if you would be okay with me attending a dinner party with one of my best friends. I know how you are about me going out after dark without you."

Knowing what lurked in the shadows and our affinity for young men or women, I often forbade Holly from roaming the streets after sunset.

Seeing the look of desperate longing on her face proved holding my resolve more difficult the longer she did so. I gave in, making her promise not to leave her friend's house alone or at all, provided she complete her chores both in the house and outside of it.

With more vigor than I would have liked, she repeated "yes" and "thank you" so many times I lost count.

"Oh! That reminds me. The groundskeeper is doing wonderfully with the gardens," Holly said with glee.

My eyes never left the paper, particularly one story involving the man from last night. "You hired a groundskeeper? I take it he has no fear of this place's reputation then?"

Holly pushed the paper down to capture my gaze with hers. "Of course he is but I promised him decent pay so he's willing to overlook it." She sauntered around me, wrapping her arms over my shoulders.

"I worry for you being alone so much. Why must you be such a recluse? I know you still hurt for Anna but--"

"That will be enough." I said. My voice a tone not to be questioned. "As far as anyone knows, I do not exist and I am more than fine with it. Finish your chores. I have a delivery for you to make before you leave. As always, be discreet."

Once again, Holly's lips pursed. She huffed, took the dishes to the kitchen and prepared to go about her daily business.

I retired to my study to ponder the story of the man's murder and Inspector Abrams' mention of another mangled corpse.

It soon became obvious, what with the memories of Anna resurfacing and my mind's endless pursuit of answers, that sleep would remain elusive.

Knocking on the door interrupted my thoughts. Holly threw it open, almost allowing it to slam against the wall.

"I almost forgot, I think Inspector Abrams' son has taken a fancy to me."

Oh dear. I thought. "And do you find yourself attracted to him?"

She shook her head.

"Then there is no need to worry. Let him down easily but be polite. The inspector has done much to dissuade the general public from their thoughts about you."

A thick silence lingered in the air.

"I heard another poor person was murdered," Holly finally said. She hesitated at the last word, her voice barely a whisper.

I kept my focus on the spire of Big Ben above the treeline.

"So I can put my heart at ease, it wasn't you, was it?" Holly asked.

"No, dearest. I do not kill unnecessarily. Now, go finish your chores and enjoy your evening. I will be out late tonight and will be checking on you." I grinned at the look of defiance on her face.

With a sigh, I lowered my head. Somewhere in my daughter's heart, she still feared me, seeing me as a monster.

III. London's New Arrival

In light of Holly spending the evening with her friend, I decided to leave the manor and drift up to one of my favorite places to overlook the city.

Big Ben provided the perfect venue for me to listen to almost all of the corners of the city. The moon shone full in the sky, her face covered by wisps of spectral clouds, creating a blurred halo. The scent of fresh snow wafted on the air, promising a new blanket.

Soft sounds of whispering winds accompanied by the night birds and bats offered a sense of peace and calm to my disturbed mind.

Smoke from industrial business stacks brought about a cringe from the burning in my lungs.

A horrifying scream rose in the quiet, ending my contemplating.

The pungent smell of blood and death penetrated my nostrils.

I followed it until I came upon another body. Only this time, she not only suffered a brutal mauling. Her eviscerated belly displayed crimson entrails for all to see. Blood pooled around the grotesque organs, its copper smell mixing with the rot of mold, stale alcohol and urine.

In light of the police, I shifted into the form of a black cat and perched on the nearby ledge of a red brick building so I could listen and observe.

Pupil-less eyes the color of ruby glistened in the dim light of the street lamps muted by thickening fog.

Officer Abrams stood scratching his head beneath his domed hat, taking it off and running a chubby hand through his thinning red mane. "I need to retire. This just keeps getting bloody worse," He said.

Another officer, a younger fellow,   looked green, ready to show what he ate for dinner.

The lad darted for the nearest corner, unable to hold it in any longer.

Abrams shook his head.

Another officer, an older man with a long handlebar mustache, joined Abrams. "In all my years, I've never seen such evil. Not even during my time in the Jack the Ripper case."

Abrams drew up his mouth and brows up. With an "ah" he added, "According to rumor, they're bringing another bloke from Brighton to help aid in solving these strange killings. Apparently, he's a detective quite versed in a new form of science. Forensics or something."

"Why so violent? What's the purpose?" The other, much taller man said.

Officer Abrams shrugged and instructed his medical examiner to give him the preliminary findings.

The young lady had not been dead long. How the police arrived so quickly puzzled me.

I guessed one of the watchmen on the corner alerted them after they heard the scream.

The examiner told me nothing of interest. Once the body got prepared to leave the scene, I stayed to listen to the conversation between the three officers.

"Constable Abrams, you know, I've been thinking. We haven't been able to find any evidence to point us to a killer and well, the other victims had their throats torn out. You don't think--" The young man's statement ended when Abrams and his partner guffawed at the top of their lungs.

Abrams' round belly bounced as he laughed. "Let me guess, some dark creature of myth who sucks blood, yes? Give me a bloody break. There's no such thing."

My eyes rolled at Abrams' ignorance. I hated that label as any other of my kind. Still, discarding a viable theory when human science could not offer a viable explanation to what happened appeared to borderline arrogance.

One might go as far as to say stupidity.

"Seriously, Officer Porter, leave such nonsense in your fiction novels. What we have here is a serial killer with an affinity for the occult." The older officer added to Abrams' statement. His pointed nose drawn up, eyes directed down its length at the young man.

Porter appeared dejected, a blush of red falling across his face as he left. I almost felt sorry for the lad.

Abrams and his fellow officer lingered a moment longer going on about this new forensic detective arriving from Brighton.

My interest remained with the body now placed in the examiner's car.

I leapt down onto the roof, keeping low to avoid being seen, wanting to get a closer look at the corpse.

Perhap my own examination would yield a scent of something other than putrid organs and blood I could track back to the killer.

* * *

We arrived at the morgue after a rather annoying and windy ride. I took the form of black mist and drifted up into the air ducts.

Once inside, I shifted into a rat to follow along the maze until I arrived at the vent overlooking the morgue.

The medical examiner and his assistant opened the black bag containing the body, their eyes widening in both disgust and shock.

Dr. Donald Farnsworth, the older of the two, worked at the morgue for as long as I had known him. We spoke in passing during those rare times I enjoyed an outing amongst humans during the day.

"Bloody hell," The doctor began. "Yet another with the throat torn to shreds. I've never seen anything like this. Have the police any leads?"

His apprentice shook his head.

"Well, it's too late to do anything tonight. Let's retire and we can continue this in the morning," Farnsworth commented.

Farnsworth helped the young man haul the body to put it in one of the freezers to perform whatever autopsy the murderer left for them to perform.

I watched the men walk out before dropping down to observe the body myself, beginning with the throat.

Though messy, the murderer hid his work by tearing all the way through the trachea and carotid arteries. The tear of the throat happened when fangs ripped through the flesh.

A subtle hint of fresh sex rose amongst the smell of gore. This murder held the clues of an act so vile it brought about great anger in me. Whenever such a crime occurred, I hunted the perpetrator and tore them apart myself.

My anger quelled a bit when another scent – faint, yet lingering – offered a clue for me to track.

I followed the ducts outside, shifted into a Great Dane and began tracing the scent. At London Bridge, it became lost amongst the smells of raw fish, salty air and smoke.

Whimpering, I sat on the cobblestone tapping my tail against the ground in frustration.

Shuffling shoes over the concrete behind me brought my attention to a young man who appeared to be lost. He had a handsome face, with sharp jaws and defined cheekbones.

Dark hair drifted down his neck, something not typical of an English gentleman of the day.

In his hand, he held a brown briefcase, in the other a hat blown by the wind almost into the channel. The tan coat he wore whipped around, giving him the look of a bumbling new arrival to London's weather.

For some reason, I found him interesting.

"Evening," He said, breath heavy at the exertion against the wind. "I appear to be a bit lost. Could you perhaps show me the way to the police station?"

To an average man, the image of someone asking a dog for directions might appear whimsical, if not foolish. Why he decided to do so, I did not understand but chose to lead him to where he wanted to go.

Tipping his hat, he walked into the station while I departed to Holly's friend's house to make sure Holly remained indoors after sunset.

I saw her laughing with her friend through the window as I perched on the branch overlooking the room. It pleased me to observe her so happy and enjoying some time with women her age.

Becoming mist, I traveled over the breeze back home to land in the garden behind the house.

My mind drifted to a memorable time when Annabelle and I enjoyed each other's company on picnics, horse rides and at times, hide and seek in the forest at night. Sometimes to tease me, she went swimming in nothing but her undergarments. The latter often ended with a pleasurable evening.

IV. Ghost Love Score

I awoke to find Holly still gone despite her promise to return early. Perturbed, I hurried my morning routine.

Debating on whether or not I should go into town and drag her back home or see if she'd been hurt, I paced the floor, growling through my teeth.

The events of the night before remained fresh in my mind, scaring me into imagining horrific scenarios.

For the longest time, Holly begged me for independence, for trust to let her stay out after dark.

When I decided to do so, my gut wrenched in my stomach to the point of making me want to vomit. Cold water in my face helped in regaining some clarity enough so I could finish getting dressed and go out to Annabelle's grave to help me relax.

Fresh snow blanketed the cobblestone paths leading through the wrought iron gate to the winding gardens.

In Anna's memory, I buried her within the garden. The death of the vibrant colors during the grey of winter always brought about a feeling of melancholy and loneliness when I visited.

Beneath the bones of the Weeping Willow, I knelt in front of the solitary marble stone, placing a rose on the small protruding lip.

Crippled vines wrapped around the stone, deadened by winter's cold. "I hope you do not mind my company, my love. My mind is a disheveled mess and this place always brings such a sense of peace."

I pulled my jacket around me, a shield against the blistering cold. I remained beneath the willow for the greater part of the day, still waiting on Holly and drifting off to sleep while reading the works of Poe.

Snow still whispered, the only sound against the silence.

* * *

London Downs
Spring, 1566

Annabelle blushed. For months, she hinted at wanting to take our relationship further. When it came down to my taking her offer, she appeared hesitant.

When I inquired as to her reason, she blushed more. "I've never done this before. My father would disown me if he learned about it."

I took the slender woman in my arms, my hands flat against her lower back, pushing her body into mine. "Anna, we do not need to do this if you want to wait. I only wanted you to know my willingness to give you what you desire."

In her eyes, I saw her mind fighting her heart. It hurt me to see her in such turmoil.

To ease her decision, I took my time in removing pieces of her clothing, offering for her to tell me to stop if she changed her mind.

Our lips met in a passionate kiss, my hands venturing over her bared back down to her clothed buttocks. Her warm, soft skin excited me, igniting an inner fire of lust.

Determination not to force her held my control in place until she began unbuttoning my shirt, pushing the fabric away to reveal my shoulders.

A bright smile and longing eyes replaced the uncertainty in Anna's gaze as she leaned forward to place gentle pecks along my collarbone to my shoulder.

It did not take long for me to lead her to lie on her back on the blanket and give her everything she wanted. Our bodies entwined beneath the shade of the tree.

My mind blurred to a point where I had no sense of whose screams belonged to whom.

Her blood sang through her veins, its heat tempting me to take it and throw Anna further into an ecstasy she would never forget.

I clenched my teeth together, choking the need.

For as long as I could, I wanted my darkness to remain hidden from the only light I had ever known in my life.

Anna probed me to find out what went through my mind. "Nothing, dearest. Let this night be about fulfilling your dreams."

I kissed her, pushing her into the soft grass, her nails gripping the muscles of my back. The idea of taking Anna so openly in our own little world excited me. Her father's rules seemed so distant, his voice of reason drowned out even for a brief moment.

The day drifted into night with me taking Anna over and over until the sweet embrace of sleep took us both beneath the moon.

* * *

Cold arms wrapping around my shoulders pulled me back from the dream. I turned half-lidded eyes to see Anna's spectral form staring back at me with a smile lit across her face.

She caressed both sides of my jaw with chilled fingertips, her hand leaving my face to reach down to unbutton the top two buttons of my shirt.

I shivered as she began to stroke my skin.

"Anna, I told you you did not have to linger here. I know you know what else lurks beneath the house."

Anna's lips puckered. She lacked the ability to speak but I knew what she wanted to say. She said it many times in all of the years she danced across the garden with such a light touch, one might mistake her for a fae.

I enjoyed watching her at night, her white form drifting over the different portions of the garden. She often looked up at me, teasing me by licking her lips or hiding behind the trunks of the trees only to take off again.

Her flowing hair drifted behind her, the thin fabric of her dress tattering into spectral mist.

She placed an icy kiss on my neck, her hand returning to cradling my jaw with the softest brush of her fingers.

Lacking a physical form, she had to be careful or she would go through me.

Anna mouthed "Love you." Our exchanges remained that way throughout the years – she with short statements, I with translating the best I could.

I rose from the ground, requesting Anna to dance for me to help ease the frustration at Holly's lateness.

Anna did so, twirling around on the balls if her feet, sometimes placing her hands on my shoulders as she circled around me. Every movement she performed exhibited panther-like grace.

In play, she tapped my ear, bringing a sense of cold enough to make me shiver.

At the end of her dance, Anna communicated she wanted to play hide and seek. I obliged her, covering my eyes and waiting for her to hide.

Detecting a ghost presented as much of a challenge as tracking mortals. My irises became those of the cat, allowing me to see through the veil to follow Anna's tracks.

They led me to the statue of an angel holding a bowl with frozen water drifting over the edge into a pool at the bottom. Lily pads sat suspended in place from the arctic at the bottom of the waterfall.

I laughed at her response when I said "Found you."

Anna moved through the snow with such haste she kicked up a white powder that hit me in the face.

I shook out my hair, complaining about how some of the snow found its way   into my shirt.

She covered a laugh and danced back off towards the willow where her gravestone lie.

Cold bit into me but I sat in the space she cleared for us and began reading some works of Robert Frost to her. He remained one of her favorite poets along with Walden and Lord Byron.

In all of our years together, it still surprised me to learn how much we had in common.

Around mid-day, hunger and fatigue forced me to bid Anna farewell, apologizing for allowing what happened to her in the past.

She shook her head, her eyes glistening with unshed tears, mouthing "Not your fault" and "Miss you."

"I miss you too," I replied and turned to retire to the warmth of the house.

V. Walter

In the confines of my study, a newly lit fire helped to warm the lingering chill of the room. Raven Hollow lacked such luxuries like electricity due to its age and my not wanting to make it look inhabited. The idea of my home being haunted was something I strove to keep in the minds of the Londoners.

In times past, children would come on dares to see if the ghosts roaming my halls existed or in only rumors and folklore.

The presence of the ghosts took care of them in my stead.

For you see, my home of Raven Hollow is indeed haunted by many ghosts..

As with Annabelle, spirits roamed the main ballroom and often take it upon themselves to play tricks despite knowing and respecting what I am. Only one remained whose hate allowed him to defy my authority, the one imprisoned beneath the manor.

"I'm home, Father!" Holly's delighted voice from the entryway of my study reminded me of the foul mood I fell into due to her tardiness. .

The sound of her piping, sweet voice calling me "father" warmed my heart. I had to look away from the door to hide a smile and adopt a chiding tone.

"And where were you? I expected you home this morning," I asked.

I watched Anna outside dancing around the willow, hiding behind the trunk, licking her lips and flirting when she saw me looking.

From behind me, I heard Holly shuffle her feet against the carpet, mumbling like I could not hear her.

"I am waiting," I demanded, placing clasped hands behind my back like a soldier standing at attention.

Holly sighed. "I'm sorry I disobeyed you. Marie and I went out last night. I met the most wonderful man."

"A young man, you say? What did this young man say or do to capture your fancy?" I turned, my eyebrow raised to find Holly's face red with blush, eyes directed away from mine and towards the floor.

She pushed her hair away from her face. "I didn't say he captured my fancy."

I could hear her heart pounding like a parade drum. Her breath hastened. The smell of sweat wafted through the air.

"Do I get to meet him?" I asked. My voice sounded more upset than I meant it to.

Holly's lower lip stuck out. Her furrowed brows and frowning mouth told me the answer.

We found ourselves engulfed in a silent stalemate.

To end it, Holly asked me how my night went.

I told her, leaving out the gory details and the rumors of bloodsucking monsters.

A look of blind terror hung in her blue eyes. "My God. The police have no idea who is doing these appalling things?"

The police only accept what mortal science can tell them. "Not yet. Officer Abrams says they plan on sending a forensic detective from Brighton to aid in the investigation."

Holly looked away then back at me. "What do you think?"

Smart girl.

When she quizzed me the first time about what I was, she asked all the normal questions a human might ask regarding the sun, running water, cold skin and a lack of a beating heart.

Oddly, for some reason, she wanted to know if we sparkled in the sun or not. The latter made no sense to me but I entertained her curiosity.

Many of those myths, I denied as false. My heart beat healthy behind warm skin and as soft a complexion of any man of the era.

Perhaps a bit more pale than the average mortal but certainly not enough to make me look dead.

A loud rapping on the doors of the manor turned our attention to the new visitor.

Holly volunteered to answer it.

I chose to remain in the shadows at the head of the stairs in the shape of the same black rat I became at the morgue. My tail curled around tiny pink paws, red beady eyes locked on the door to see the groundskeeper.

Sensitive ears allowed me to hear what they said.

"Evening, Miss Holly." The groundskeeper took off his hat for the greeting. His grey beard and bushy grey eyebrows hid small eyes beneath defined cheekbones and sunken sockets. "There's a detective wishing to speak to the Master of the house. I tried telling him I hadn't seen a master but he insists."

Holly thanked the groundskeeper, glancing at me, awaiting my reply before instructing the elderly man to let the detective in.

To my surprise, the same man from night before walked through my front doors, soaked from the deluge outside.

Thunder shook the house, a strange occurrence for a London winter.

"Oh my, it's you!" Holly exclaimed.

As they exchanged banter, it soon became apparent how much interest they had in each other.

"I need to speak with the master of the mansion," the detective, whom I learned to be named Walter Deverough, said. "Does he live here or does he manage the property from elsewhere?"

"The owner lives here but he doesn't usually take kindly to unannounced guests," Holly replied.

After being informed of "official business" I returned to my study, shifting back into my more human form to wait for the two to join me..

Holly came through the door.

I cut her off before she had the chance to say anything. "You need not ask, send him in."

She left with a curt "yes" only to return with the detective in tow. I sat turned away from the desk, hidden from the detective's view, legs crossed, hands clasped on my knees.

Frustration niggled the back of my mind at the intrusion, yet I remained eager to discover how the detective learned of my existence.

"That is close enough, Detective." I said, wanting it to be known I held no appreciation of his uninvited appearance nor his interest in my daughter.

"Forgive my intrusion, I have a few questions." I heard him rustling in the same tan coat he wore the night before. "I found this letter on my front porch this morning. It mentions how you might know of what's been going on in."

I creased my brows together, closing my eyes. *A letter? It mentions me?*

Earlier theories rose in the forefront in my mind. *No, it cannot be. She could not have survived.*

Walter cleared his throat, his feet shuffling on the floor.

I opened my eyes, rings of bright silver illuminated the heavy shades of the fading light of the day.

Though I knew more than I let on, I had no interest in wanting to share what I knew.

"I know nothing more than any other bloke in London, sir. I must say I do not appreciate such accusations," I said, making sure the detective heard the disdain and insult.

Questions erupted from Walter's mouth faster than I believed even he knew.

The longer the interrogation went on, the more eager I grew to get this man out of my house.

Things became strange when Walter suddenly stopped, clearing his throat and allowing the room to fall into silence.

"Thank you for your time. If I may, sir, there is one last thing, though I regret this might not be an opportune time to ask." Another throat clearing. "Will you allow me the honor of seeing your daughter? For nothing more than to enjoy the company of a beautiful woman."

Feral anger allowed the beast to come through. I wanted to tear the man's throat out at the audacity he showed in accusing me of murder then to dare to ask for my daughter's time.

I ordered him to leave.

Walter's eyes betrayed the hint of fear I saw within them. He thanked me, turned and left the room.

The sound of his shoes disturbing the carpet out into the hall, followed by the slamming of the front doors assured me of Walter's departure.

Outside, pounding rain continued to fall. An echo of the mood I could sense growing within the room.

VI. "You're A Monster"

Anger still blistered inside of me when Holly returned from seeing Walter to the door. I watched out of the window, careful to remain unseen when the detective glanced back up towards the house.

I heard Holly stomping the wood in the hallway despite the runner spanning the length of it. I could hear her huffing behind me before she even spoke.

"You didn't have to be so cross with him! He only came here to do his job!"

"That is enough. He came here to accuse me of murder and dared ask for your hand." I said, unyielding.

My words did little to hinder her from throwing accusations back at me. "I am not a child anymore, Jonathan! Is your intent to keep me here until you choose to turn your darker nature on me too?"

Her last words wounded me as though they were made with a blade of pure silver. I clenched sharpened canines, turning on my heel.

My hands hit the wooden desktop, jostling pens and knocking over plastic containers. "I said that is enough! How dare you speak to me like this? You have already shown me I cannot trust you to come home when you promised. As long as I live, you will not go anywhere near Walter Deverough again. Do you understand me?"

I tried my best to keep from scaring her but from the trembling I saw in my daughter's eyes and the subtle shaking of her hands, I knew I failed.

Her shoulders drew up, tears formed in the corners of her eyes. "You're a monster!" Holly fled down the hallway and slammed the door of her room.

Monster. I lowered my head, eyes focused on the ink dripping over the edges of the accusing letter Walter gave to me.

The scathing words glared back. I cared less at the moment when I thought about how I lost precious control and startled my daughter.

Monster. The word echoed over and over in my head.

I smashed a fist down on the desktop, cursing myself for snapping at both Holly and Walter.

Outside, rain pattered against the panes of the window, wind whipped the branches of the trees forcing them to scratch against the panes, whining beneath the force of the gale. I could hear the squeaking of the gate attached to the brick wall bordering the confines of Raven Hollow.

I chose to retire to take a hot bath to calm my fraying nerves, taking the letter and reading it repeatedly.

In scrawled ink written with a quilled pen, I read the words addressed to Walter outlining how the master of Raven Hollow knew more about the murders. It outlined how I hid behind a facade and told lies about my true nature.

Walter neglected to mention anything about the latter which surprised me.

Warm water against aching joints helped ease the stress and I sank further into the bath, exhaling a deep breath to calm myself.

The pain from Holly's words and the fear in her eyes pierced my heart.

I decided to try to patch things up as best I could before the night ended so I could hopefully get some peace.

Scars marred my skin from years of fighting both my own kind and the hunters who sought to destroy us.

One jagged scar lined the extent of my back, from the shoulder down to the hip. Another, shorter scar crossed over it forming the shape of a cross. It served as a reminder of the sins I still paid for and the repentance I longed to have.

Sighing, I rose from the water, got out of the porcelain bath and proceeded to dry myself off.

It never mattered what I wore to bed since I often chose to sleep with nothing on at all.

I ran my hands through my hair while staring at the mirror, my complexion more pale than usual, eyes dark with the lingering hunger I needed to fulfill. *I suppose I should address it after trying to speak with Holly.*

I dressed and left the bathroom.

* * *

Holly's door appeared daunting as I stood staring at it. I rested my forehead against the ivory wood, heart pounding with fear that Holly would not speak to me.

I tapped on it, hoping Holly would answer. "Dearest, please forgive me. I should not have acted so rashly. Things have been stressful as of late."

No sound came from the other side. "Holly?" I tried the doorknob to find it locked.

I decided to let the situation calm itself and try again in the morning.

Returning to my study, I sat in the oscillating chair, legs crossed, fingers interlocked over my mouth.

The damning letter stared back at me on the desk. Only when I allowed my temper to fully cool down did I become aware of the faint smell of a woman's perfume permeating my nostrils.

Impossible. My eyes bulged almost fully white when the haunting scents of daffodils and balsam intermingled.

Shoving the chair away, I grabbed the letter and whipped around, my coat tails flapping as I threw the letter into the fire.

Quickened breaths escaped my lungs, sweat beaded across my forehead made worse by the tousled bangs of my hair. *She cannot be. This. This cannot be.*

Every horrible memory I could think of intruded my mind at one time.

The night of the first Great Fire responsible for almost razing Nottingham to the ground flashed across my frontal lobe.

Shadowed lips dripping poisonous words brought tickles across my skin as though *she* lingered in the room around me like a demon not willing to be put to rest.

I could feel the gentle traces of her nails, hear her toxic whispers. Everything reminding me of *her* rammed into me all at once.

Had I the capability, I would have vomited.

This darkness I could feel haunting London's streets just as the infamous fog sent my soul into a discord more powerful than the malice beneath the mansion.

No sleep would come for me that night. I decided to do something I despised and took the winds of the departing storm.

VII. Body In the Alley

The wind made it difficult but I managed to float across the channel, watching the lights flashing on the ships coming in and out. Loud chimes warning people to be mindful of the rising bridge echoed, joining Big Ben's deep booming voice.

Smoke stacks billowing in the cool night air did nothing to hinder the full moon from emerging behind the departing clouds. The shining glow of night's goddess always did well to calm me against the chaos within my soul.

By the time I hit the cobblestone streets of London, the rain became a gentle trickle of drops to the ground. A cold wind kept the fog from thickening to its usual density.

Nights like these made hunting difficult since everyone remained indoors. I meandered around for a bit, searching.

As luck would have it, the daughter of the local seamstress emerged from her mother's shop, locking the door. She turned towards the sidewalk, her eyes on the ground.

I watched her round the corner bookshop to the alleyway leading to an old building with lofts where residents shared a single washroom.

Shifting into mist, I moved in front of her, changing back and allowing her to bump into me.

She stumbled. I reached out and caught her around the waist.

"Oh dear!" She said. "Forgive me, I wasn't watching--" The words froze when her eyes fell on me.

I smiled, offering a slight laugh. "It is quite alright. I should have been more aware. I hope you were not hurt."

The young woman stuttered, her cheeks a deep red. Dark auburn curls fell over her shoulders in waves, petite hands brushing them away from her face. Bright eyes offset the darkness of her hair.

Guilt plagued me for what I had to do.

I helped her straighten to standing, the guilt shifting to the enjoyment that crept within me the further she fell under my dark influence.

A villain relishes the moment his prey submits to his power, I am no different.

My fingertips brushed her jaw as I pushed her against the nearest brick wall of the alley.

Thudding heartbeats pushed sweet rivers of blood rushing through her veins. I could smell the scent of her as want became lust.

I placed my arm around her slowly, murmuring sweet words to her, lulling her deeper into my embrace.

Hunger caused the tips of my canines to burn the closer I came to her throat.

"I will not hurt you, sweet one," I said, placing tender kisses on her jaw, down the length of the slender cream of her skin of her throat.

A small gasp escaped the woman's lips when my fangs pierced her flesh. My tongue lapped up the rubies of her lifeblood flowing steadily from the puncture marks. I took my time, allowing the narcotic saliva coax her body to surrender more of its delicious essence to satiate a creature of the shadows.

"Your name, dear one. Tell it to me," I said in a seductive tone, my thumb tracing the strawberry of her lips.

She stuttered, moaning and pressing her body into mine. "B-Beth."

I smiled, repeating it, returning to feeding while Beth's hands tangled in my hair.

* * *

The sound of a night owl, songs of crickets and croaking frogs served as my companions while I walked the empty streets.

Another bout of rain arrived in the wee hours of the morning, soaking me to the bone. I did not wish to go home out of concern Holly might still be awake and question me about where I'd been.

Sitting at a bench in the park, I drew my jacket up.

Folklore and literature did their best to make us out to be something almost laughable. Of course, I did not exist in the same labels as many who lurked in the night and took blood to live.

My hunger went beyond such trivial needs.

Whereas others could drink the blood of the dead, lacked a heartbeat and possessed skin as cold as ice, I could not partake of the blood of the dead.

A heart had to pump fresh, warm blood or it made me ill to the point of death in large enough doses. I also had the option to neglect blood altogether and feed on sexual energy if I chose.

The latter often proved rare since I preferred to see women as more than sexual companions.

I had done so a few times in my life and the satisfaction surpassed blood by kilometers. However, choosing respect over ecstasy separated me from being a deviant in my eyes.

Silence took hold for what felt like hours until the scent of death drifted in the breeze. *It has happened again. I wonder who the poor unfortunate soul is this time.*

I drifted into mist, following the scent to another alley three blocks away from the park. The police had not arrived so I decided to drop down onto the soaked ground and explore the scene.

Rotten meat, alcohol, smoke and heaven only knew what else all intertwined. The sickening cocktail caused my stomach to lurch.

My eyes searched the darkness.

I gasped when I recognized the alley connecting Beth's loft to the main street. *Oh God, no. Please no.*

Fear became panic when I tracked the scent to the open windows of Beth's loft. The sight that befell my eyes caused them to widen, my heart sinking.

Beth lay on her bed, legs sprawled out, her eyes devoid of life, throat torn open. She smiled, moaning in delight a few short hours ago.

Leaning over her body, my tears fell onto her cheek. I whispered "I am so sorry" into her ear. My fingers fell over her eyes like the man I found at the start of all of this hell, closing them.

I drifted into my grief, neglecting to notice when Detective Walter Deverough filled the doorway, his terrified eyes locked on me.

From the first floor, I heard the shuffling of boots, announcing the arrival of the other police officers.

Minutes passed while we stared at one another. I waited for him to sound the alarm, not wanting to fight or harm anyone in an attempt to escape.

"Detective!" A voice called from downstairs. It sounded like Abrams. "We're coming up!"

My heart thudded dizzying me. I covered my lips with my finger-tip, shaking my head. Walter called down to Abrams to give him a moment, signaling with a waving hand for me to run.

I nodded, leaping from the window out into the night.

VIII. An Unexpected Patient

I made it to the edge of the woods leading up to Raven Hollow. Hastened breath escaped my lungs at recalling the look on Walter's face when he saw me. My mind swam with thoughts of what I must have looked like leaning over the mangled body of the young woman on the bed.

I cursed under my breath, fangs clenching, nails digging into the thick trunk of the old oak leading up to the now hidden path to my self-imposed prison.

For as long as I could remember, I valued the silence the mansion granted me. In reality it served as an asylum for a soul cursed by wickedness.

At times I would walk the woods, hearing the subtle whispers of the dead. Not those created by the hate of the serial killers of London's crimson past but of my own making.

Bare branches creaked, whined and moaned in the wind, whipping crumpled leaves around like corpses turned to husks by time. The ground turned foul over the years, a result of the evil of the malice locked away within the mansion.

Even being so far away, I could feel the pressure of the demon's presence. It saturated everything around it despite being sealed in a coffin chained closed by blessed silver.

Images of Beth's face frozen in death's icy grip gripped my chest so strongly, it took the very breath out of me.

Cree. My nails tore at the bark of the oak, splintering wood, bringing about lifeblood which dripped down my fingers to the sleeve of my black coat.

Falling to my knees, I raised my head, screaming to the heavens, bloodied fists clenched at my sides. Rings of angry silver replaced the natural color of my irises – hate radiated from me at my existence.

Many innocent souls – Annabelle, Beth – and many more like them had already died because of my shortcomings.

I stared at the moon, eyes large with realization. *Someone who wanted to see me suffer.*

It made every suspicion, every theory spin out of control in my mind.

All of the murders were centered around me.

Someone who hated me enough to pay for their crimes - someone who wanted to cause as much pain as they could probably before coming after me themselves - had been watching me.

I thought about the letter Walter brought to my attention. *It cannot be. But who else could it be?*

Pounding rain replaced the flurries of snow, soaking me as I hung my head staring at the heavy drops hitting the ground.

I rose to my feet, refusing to take the form of the black mist in exchange for taking a long, tempered walk through the woods.

* * *

The morning following the awful murder, I woke to find the house disturbingly empty. From the brightness of the rays beneath the black curtains in my chamber, I could tell I overslept.

Strange. Holly should have already tried to awaken me by now. I hurried to dress and leave my room to head for Holly's.

No foreign scents or feelings lingered in the air so I knew she had not been abducted. I reached her room to find the door wide open, the thick blankets of her bed already made up.

Many in the town thought her a witch since she lived in a house full of restless spirits, some calling "the mansion's mysterious master" a demented soul for allowing a child to live there.

Strangely enough, the ghosts never bothered Holly and my many attempts to get her to live in the servant's house met with open defiance. She   appeared to enjoy the company of the spectral interlopers. They never disturbed her so I let the matter go.

To find her gone brought about a sense of terror I had not known in many years. I roamed the room, searching for any clue to where she might have gone.

My eyes fell upon an envelope tucked beneath the silver brush I purchased for her when she asked for her first vanity. I took it and tore it open to read the message written in Holly's delicate hand.

Jonathan,

I want to thank you for everything you have done but I cannot stay in a place where I am treated like a child. I love you more than anything but I must be allowed to live my own life. You had no right to treat Walter in such a despicable manner. In light of your revealing of your more monstrous nature, I am leaving. Please do not seek me out. Nothing will change my love for you, Father.

Your ever loving daughter,
Holly

Tears dripped onto the cream paper. I lifted my hand to trace it along my cheek.

In my many years of life, only a few events brought about such an emotional reaction. My fingers trembled as I stared at them, confused and hurt at her referral of my "more monstrous nature."

Again, I fell to my knees, damning myself for allowing such a lapse in control. Everything spiraled further into chaos the longer I let these murders occur near my home.

Monster. The word mulled in my mind like souring whiskey left to brew too long.

I resigned myself to my study to continue writing, waiting for the sun to set so I could watch Anna dancing in the garden, listen to her haunting song she sang.

* * *

Twilight the following evening found me wandering through the halls of the mansion, down the stairs, my fingers tracing the redwood of the rails.

Pushing the double doors open, I stepped out into the pattering rain to the garden where Anna met me beneath the willow.

"I am losing her, Anna. Losing myself." Anna sat on her knees beside me, hugging me around the head. "I...am scared." The words came out in a hushed breath.

A voice above the rain and wind drew our moment to a close. Holly scrambled around one of the hedges, her presence making Anna retreat to avoid any unwanted questions.

Gasping, eyes large, I got to my feet in time to receive my daughter in my arms. "Holly, thank the night you are safe." She looked up at me sobbing. "What is it, dear one?"

"Please! He's hurt!" Holly said.

"Who?"

"Walter! Please, you have to help him?"

I wasted no time in following her to the front porch where Walter Deverough sat against the front doors. His chest heaved, his hand gripping a wound in his side streaming with blood, staining his beige coat.

On the side of his head, I saw a cut dripping with blood down his face. One of his eyes had begun to swell, forcing it to nearly close.

Whatever did this to him stopped before killing him unless he barely escaped. I doubted the latter.

With brows creased, a deep scowl on my face, I asked Holly what happened, helping Walter to his feet and taking him into the house.

IX. Her Lips Were Still Red

Holly threw open the doors of the guest room to allow me to come through with Walter, his blood dripping onto the rug.

I laid the Detective down, tearing the tattered remains of his coat and shirt away to survey the extent of his wounds.

"By the night," I said.

The wound in Walter's side gaped, the flesh torn. It reminded me of blood red lips, each side split like with a surgeon's blade.

I scowled. No blade had done this.

Holly hesitated when I told her to leave and get the medical supplies from my bathroom. I imagined it to be because of her concern of my darker side.

"Now! He will die!" My harsh tone snapped Holly from her delusion.

Nodding, she fled, returning, carrying the supplies and setting them down on the bedside table.

I hastened in unbuttoning my sleeves, rolling them up so I could go to work on Walter's wounds.

The scent of his fresh blood made the beating of his heart all the louder in my sensitive ears. It teased my carnal senses, pleading with me to sink my fangs into his throat and lap up the delicious nectar of his life. I shoved the thoughts away to focus on saving the man my daughter had come to love.

Holly paced the room, tears streaming, sniffling and uttering tender muted prayers beneath her voice. "Please be okay, please God, let him be okay."

It wounded me to see her becoming more of a young woman, ready to leave the sanctity of Raven Hollow to spread her wings into the world of passion and romance. Again, I pushed the thoughts away. I knew the day would come when she would leave but nothing could have prepared me for when it happened.

Walter screamed in pain as I started to sew the wound closed.

To calm him, I let the seduction of my kind sink into him, whispering for him to relax and deceiving his mind into thinking he felt no pain. Soon, he settled, whimpering when I pierced his flesh with the hooked needle and pulled the thread through.

Holly settled in a chair she pulled up beside the bed and took Walter's hand, putting it to her face and humming a gentle tune.

Once I finished, I cleaned and covered the wound with gauze and medical tape.

Walter settled into slumber.

I had to step away to regain control of the raging hunger causing the tips of my fangs to erupt in biting flames. Nothing compared to the torment of one of my kin being subjected to hours of blood-letting and being unable to partake of such an easy prize.

To describe the experience, I needed words not known to the language of mortals.

"Jonathan," Holly whispered from behind me. Her hand lay on my shoulder-blade, followed by her warm cheek. "Your heart is pounding."

The side of my fist met the wall, fangs grinding in hate for what I wanted to do.

I almost threw away what Holly would think of me and tore into Walter, taking everything he had until he no longer moved.

For centuries, I denied my true nature – the demon longing to feed on sexual passion and blood. I only sipped from my victims, leaving my body above starving.

My back began to rumble when Holly started humming and rubbing my shoulder-blade in reassuring circles. A smile replaced the grinding fangs, the hate melting into love at seeing and feeling my daughter's understanding of how much I suffered.

She thanked me for what I did for the one she loved. "I know it must have been hard."

I heaved out a heavy breath through my nostrils, eyes closing to relax the beast within me. "You are...fond of him."

No reply came immediately, followed by a passionate sigh. "Is this what it feels like? To be in love, I mean. Is this how you felt when you met Anna?"

My heart froze, a slight gasp escaping my throat. Surprised eyes locked on the floral wallpaper in front of me.

"Why have you never told me what happened? The reason you have been so sad and isolated all these years," Holly asked, her voice near to a sigh.

"It does not have a happy ending, dearest," I replied.

She repeated her question when I turned to meet the fiery eyes she often held when she accused me of treating her like a child.

"Very well. I will tell you my story."

* * *

The Hills Outside of London

1565

The afternoon sun shone over the hills overlooking the bustling London harbor. The sound of the bells chiming signaling the rising of the bridge to let another trade ship drift into the waterway.

A breeze whipped the grass in such ways that it changed from green to a golden green back to its natural shade.

Spring flowers had begun to bloom, their sweet smells drifting on the breeze, adding to the calming peace of the day.

A sharp elbow in my ribs took me from my daydreams. Wincing, I looked beside me to see Anna holding a strawberry between her thumb and two fingers.

"Jonathan Holloway, you are always such a dreamer." By the tone in her voice, she appeared to be scolding me.

As I opened my mouth to offer a rebuttal, she touched my lips with the strawberry, running it over them with half-lidded, longing eyes.

Anna's sensuality remained one of her most endearing features. My heart thumped, my mouth opening to let her tease my longing tongue with the fruit.

Speaking gently, Anna pushed it into my mouth, allowing me to take a bite, savoring its sweet, tangy mixture.

She stood from the ground, cutting off her flirting and running down the hill.

So much like her. *I thought and got up to join her in the sun.*

Late afternoon brought with it the onset of a sudden spring storm. We returned to the carriage to begin our return to her home.

We laughed, reveling in the afternoon's events, talking about what we could possibly do when we got to Anna's home.

The jerking halt of the carriage startled both of us.

"What's going on?" Anna asked. Her frightened eyes searching outside the small, curtained window.

I told her I did not know. I instructed Anna to stay in the carriage while I departed to see what happened.

At first, all seemed quiet until I saw the driver of the carriage leaning over, his hands loosened on the reigns.

I called out to him to see if he had been alright. When I moved closer, I could see his eyes remained open, his throat torn to shreds, blood pooling down his scarf onto his lap.

Anger bubbled in my chest at the realization of what happened.

Snuffing of horses in front of me – not those of the carriage – but those standing a mere nine meters away caught my attention.

Four men – no, not men – but those of my kind stood in front of their horses.

One of them, a young man with rust-toned hair, a derby hat on his head, called out to me. *"Finally, found you. Took us a damned bloody long time, you pompous bastard."*

"Found me?" I called in reply. "Do I know you, sir? Are you the one who harmed this innocent man?" I gestured to the carriage.

All four of the men chuckled, soon silenced by the one with the rust hair.

Behind me I heard screaming, bringing my attention to another man standing beside the carriage.

Unlike the others, he wore dark, formal attire. From the way the others reacted, I knew he held command over the pack.

Anna struggled against the new arrival's arm around her waist. She cried out to me, her pain rending my heart asunder at finding her amidst something I never told her about.

The man murmured in her ear, loud enough I could hear him. "Shh. I must speak with your lover. We have unfinished business he and I."

Unfinished business? I did not know the man from Adam. "Who are you? What do you want here?"

The newcomer "tsked." He stroked Anna's hair and neck, lowering to inhale her scent, closing his eyes.

It all sickened me with jealousy in such a way, I forgot his cohorts. They fell upon me, hitting and kicking me until I fell to the ground.

"That's enough. I want him conscious for this. Raise him." The leader said to his men.

I felt myself hauled to my knees under my arms, my hair fisted, forcing my eyes to look up. My ribs burned with needles of pain, my stomach nauseated and threatening to empty itself all over the rain-soaked ground.

"Jonathan Holloway, Catalina sends her regards." The leader said.

I gasped, eyes enlarged at the sound of the name.

I did not understand what happened but found myself screaming "No" at the top of my lungs. The leader spun Anna around to face him and sank his teeth deep into her throat.

She choked and gagged, turning her head to let her eyes meet mine, hand reaching out to me, gurgling something under her breath.

Her life faded from her eyes, drifting away like the streams of crimson staining the pastel blue of her dress.

The monster dropped her to the ground, took out a kerchief and proceeded to wipe the blood from his mouth. He grinned a wicked, proud grin, glowering over me.

Something snapped inside.

A rage like none I had ever felt before overtook my senses, primal strength pulsing through me. I rose from the ground, grabbed the nearest man and dug my fangs into his throat, tearing it away.

While holding him in my fangs, I ripped and tore his body parts from him, tossing them aside.

The carnage continued until nothing but dismembered limbs and ravaged throats of all four of my kind lay strewn on the dirt road, their blood mixing with the rain.

My eyes locked on the leader. He remained unshaken despite what I just did. "Impressive. But this is not over."

I flew at him, blinded by the fury, swinging elongated claws only to miss time and time again. The man escaped but not without a horrendous scar across his face.

Focusing back on Anna, I knelt beside her, pulling her into my embrace and sobbing bitter tears. I could hear no heartbeat, no breath flowed in her lungs, her blood stalled in her veins. It all happened so swiftly.

One moment I heard her laugh. The next her screams of terror.

Agony rendered me petrified, rocking the corpse of my lover and begging her to come back. Reality did not occur to me until the sun set and darkness fell. Hate and vengeance replaced the love and passion I experienced.

I vowed to find the monster who killed my Annabelle and torture him until I grew bored, then I would take my time killing him, relishing every moment.

X. Raven Hollow

Delving back into the darkest memory of my long life left a bitter taste in my mouth. I could recall what it felt like using my fangs to tear flesh of bone, taste the pungent taste of the blood of my kind – or rather, those lower on the evolutionary chain.

The hairs on my arms and back of my neck bristled at the memory of the cold air and rain after the men took my jacket off and threw me into the mud.

I did not feed like I should.

Being with Anna changed many things about me, despite my keeping the secret from her. I knew the dangers of "sipping" but gave no care as long as I could be with Anna.

Sniffling and crying took me back to Holly standing in front of me. I told her the story I never told anyone, knowing the weight of it could hurt her.

She threw her arms around my chest, holding me taut against her. "You poor thing. My God, how horrible. To lose someone you love in such a terrible way."

Her words touched my heart. I hugged her back, shushing her and petting her hair, assuring her I would be alright and had been since she came into my life. "Go. Be with the man you love. You never know if life will turn as it did with me."

I stroked my daughter's cheek, my thumb brushing away a stray tear. Placing a tender kiss on her forehead, I gestured towards the guest room, mouthing "Go."

Holly hugged me once more, placing her own kiss on my cheek, returning to her lover's bedside.

My brows furrowed in unease and disgust at remembering the name the murderer spoke that dark day - a name so wicked and evil - the sensation of being poisoned ran through my veins.

Catalina.

For centuries, I thought I eluded her and found peace within the sanctity of London.

I should have known better.

She warned me she would never stop hunting me.

At the first call of the night owl, the sounds of the spirits in the halls of Raven Hollow grew more audible.

Some of them greeted me as their master, welcoming me home despite my not leaving the whole afternoon.

Their countless nights of praise occurred like a religious ceremony with each rise and fall of the moon.

A cacophony of "My dark lords" and "Prince of the nights" grew tiresome night after night but they drowned out the loneliness after Holly went to sleep.

As I have mentioned, to many, Raven Hollow held an evil past.

In a single night, its master went mad and slaughtered every living soul with a rusted ax.

No one knew why.

No evidence could be found. What better place for one of my kind to find solitude. What better place to contain a vengeance so venomous it became a plague after death.

The baritone knell of the old grandfather clock at the base of the winding stairs tolled the midnight hour - the hour of monsters and creatures of the night.

Like one of the ghosts and as I had many times, I roamed the halls, feeling the spirits watching me. A vigil I kept to keep the grounds safe from those who might want to cause me or my daughter harm.

* * *

7 days later

I heard Walter stumble out of the guest room from behind the open door of my study. My eyes rolled out of agitation to learn he once again tried the foolish endeavor despite my many times of warning him to stay in bed.

Already, I re-stitched his side twice and chided him each time he tried to walk down the stairs.

"I can't help myself. Staying in bed so bloody long is next to being stuck in hell," he groaned, lying back on the pillow after seeing the stern glare in my eyes. "What happened, Jonathan? The girl? That thing?"

Walter rambled on and on, question after question. I had to threaten him to get him to be quiet.

"Perhaps if you told me more of what happened yourself, dear Detective, I could be more clear in answering what you want."

Taking a breath, Walter raised himself on his elbows, leaning against the headboard of the bed.

He described the night he and Holly went to the theatre, leaving out none of the gruesome details Holly had when she remained hysterical. "I've never seen anything like it. It looked like a man but I knew it wasn't."

A ghoul; a monster created when one of my kind drains not only the blood but the soul from a mortal, enthralling them to do our bidding.

Some of them became filled with a ravaging thirst and hunger; one they can never fill no matter how much they eat and drink. It is the final atonement and torture for a mortal who comes across one of my kin who wishes immortality.

Many of them resembled a man or woman with pallid flesh and sunken in features. They have no memory of being human and often do all they can to be set free from their ravenous hunger.

I encountered many in my long life, using some of my own in a bygone past. It entertained me to turn mortals into ghouls, having them beg to finish what I started to end their terrible thirst.

It all ended once I met Annabelle. I killed the ghouls who served me out of mercy.

"Forgive my bluntness but what are you? Holly told me of your history but you don't look nearly old enough to be her father," Walter asked.

My eyes lowered to the garden beneath the paned windows.

The pale light of the evening danced amidst the trees, creating shadows across the cobblestone. "I see no reason to keep this hidden any longer since you have had this encounter. I am a monster wearing the skin of a man."

An array of questions ran across Walter's eyes when I glanced at him out of my peripheral vision. I continued, hands clasped at my lower back, eyes returned to the garden below. "We are not so different, Detective. My kind and man. We can both be monstrous and war over territory, status, wealth and mates."

Walter spoke of blood-drinking monsters of lore, asking if they actually existed and if I could be labeled as one of them.

Calling me one of those lower legends of folklore fell into the same category as labeling all fruits as apples no matter where they come from.

I hated the label man's literature placed on my kind, even those who had no respect for mortals. To do so both angered and insulted.

Not all of my kind are the same.

For one, there is a caste system.

At the bottom are those we enthralled – ghouls, half-changed and what we called bleeders. At the very top are the true nobles - creatures who can ignore the need for blood and feed on intense emotions – such as sex or passionate love.

Anna's staring at me from the cobblestone, waving and pointing her arms wrenched me from my frustration. Her eyes held the air of distress.

I excused myself from Walter and descended the stairs to the front walkway.

"Anna!" I called out, my eyes taking in the details of the landscape. Something felt wrong, the air thick with a malicious presence.

The smell of rotten flesh flew on the breeze, nauseating me, reminding me of carrion left on the heated streets during the summer months.

It took me a moment to gather my wits before getting hit by something moving at great speeds.

Before me stood the writhing form of a ghoul. Despite its small stature, its speed allowed it to cause enough damage to send me bending at the waist.

Its eyes sunk so deeply into its eye sockets, the irises nothing more than spots in a pool of black. The jaw dangled, its tongue lulling like a whip ready to lash out. Skin stretched tight like a canvas allowed the ribcage to show beneath the ashen flesh.

The way it moved reminded me of a creature of folklore known as a Rake or a Skinwalker – bent over and sitting like a chimpanzee.

Slight twitches of the head and eyes added to the already pathetic visage staring back at me. The smell of rotting flesh and death lingered in the air around it.

You poor thing. How long you must have suffered. I wanted to end the thing's pain, to let it rest in peace but I needed something first. *You will lead me to your master. Then and only then, will I end your agony.*

Unwilling to shed its disgusting blood on my property, I flew past it, running at my top immortal speed into the forest.

The ghoul quickly caught up and kept pace alongside me. Such speeds were something unheard of in all of the ghouls I encountered.

Sliding behind a tree, I shifted into the form of the black rat, scuttling beneath the roots and allowing my nostrils to take in the subtle hint of the ghoul's master - or rather mistress.

Angry, the ghoul let out a screech, twirling around and hissing. "Noooossss. Wheresssss? Wheressssss?" Its head dropped, drool dripping from its tongue to the ground. "Angry....isssss. Missssstressss...."

Sickening snapping of bones and tearing of flesh ensued as the ghoul resumed a form indicative of a man.

From the way he looked and smelled, I knew without a doubt, I found Holly's attacker.

Instead of turning into mist, I decided to run the length of the forest, staying on the ghoul's scent trail.

XI. She Is My Sin

Tracking the ghoul took me to the most squalid of London's docks. Remains of fish from the markets lay strewn over the stone walkways, their foul decay polluting the air and water. Tinkling of bells echoed in the distance followed by rattling of ship tackle rustling in the light breeze of the early evening. Ocean waves capped against the harbor wall and gulls crying out added to the music of the harbor.

Docks. Why must it always be the docks? I thought, creeping through the shadows, stopping to taste the air to make sure I remained on the right path.

The strength of the odor of rot grew more profound the closer I got, soon interrupted by the bouquet of a woman's cologne.

Thick fog formed across the water, lowering visibility. Its arrival ominous, almost foreshadowing the event soon to follow.

I smelled her at first, cursing under my breath for losing the diligence utilized during the hunt for the ghoul. Her familiar perfume held the same floral aroma as the first night I smelled it. Hints of rose and balsam floated on the breeze, mixing with the odor of dead fish and refuse of the water. It might have made me sick had I not been so angry.

The click-clack of what I could only assume to be heeled shoes echoed in the brick overhang, making it sound like it came from every corner of the dock.

"Good evening, dearest." A silken, poisonous voice flowed from the woman behind me.

My breath stilled upon hearing the voice belonging to the one responsible for so much lost life. I spun on my heel to stare into the gold eyes of the evil woman, stepping back, wondering if I should run.

Before I could act, Catalina drew close to me and placed a hand on my hip, bringing about a slight flinch.

My eyes fell upon a woman who remained the same as the first time I saw her at a masquerade in the 1400s.

Deep amber waves of hair sat tight in a bun in the middle of her skull, the rest cascading in curls down to the middle of her back.

As she had done the first night we met, Catalina wore an all black ensemble save for the crimson of her gloves. Where the typical English noble chose layered skirts and dresses, Catalina wore what could only be described as the feminine style a jockey might wear.

It did not surprise me as she often chose to handle affairs personally instead of allowing those who served her to do so. I suddenly felt foolish for falling for such a trap.

The urge to kill her, to tear her to pieces and throw them into the harbor, welled up in my mind.

Because of my choices since meeting Anna, I lacked the adequate strength to do so. It could be fatal to let Catalina know such a thing. Had she chosen to, she could rip me apart slowly and enjoyed the torture.

Catalina reached out her hand to brush the back of her fingers across my cheekbone.

Try as I might, my false sense of pride did not sway her. "Jonathan, you are still as beautiful as the night I first saw you. You look hungry, darling. Could it be the rumors I heard about you are indeed true?"

Of course she knows. I let out a deep sigh.

The situation grew more dangerous for me the longer I allowed her to stay close.

To my greatest regret, Catalina knew about me in the days preceding Anna. She knew how brutal I could be, how cold and heartless I used to be.

To see me now, she could exploit such weakness. Something I could not allow her to do.

For centuries I thought her dead – burned in the flames of the Beauclair estate in 1432. To see her standing in front me baffled and terrified me.

"Why are you here?" I asked.

Catalina took out a cigarette suspended on a long plastic piece. Her shaded lips appeared to barely touch the thing, yet a billow of smoke escaped her lips, her eyes half-lidded. "Must you ask?"

Thoughts of the accursed creature beneath Raven Hollow invaded my mind. The remnants of Ezra Campion – the murderer, Catalina's former lover, the man who framed me and nearly got me killed – remained entombed in a coffin beneath my mansion. Setting him free would release a plague more deadly than any mankind would ever see.

As if she knew my thoughts, Catalina assured me her reasoning for being in London were not what I believed them to be. She cared nothing for the monster, claiming he could decay into dust in his well-deserved prison.

With no fear of what I might do or say, Catalina closed the distance between us.

Wrapping her hand around the back of my neck, she lowered my head to whisper in my ear. "My darling, what I am here for..."

My eyes widened in disbelief at what she whispered.

In a gust of freezing mix of fog and wind, I found myself alone with disturbing thoughts.

Everything I believed beginning from finding the first body no longer mattered.

Theories shattered, replaced by a fact I wished I never knew.

Reality separated from fantasy, settling into and eventually causing the realization of Catalina being alive to impact me in such a way, it nauseated me.

Instead of returning home, I chose to walk the night. The cool breeze and damp fog aided in relieving the heated stress of my encounter, no matter how brief.

Memories of regret and guilt flooded my consciousness. *If only I never attended the Ball.*

* * *

All Hallow's Eve

1430

The night of the Masquerade saw some of the most beautiful and elegant gowns. Coaches of all shapes, sizes and colors bore the nobility and those who served them to the Beauclair Estate to enjoy a night unhindered by superstition. Women held onto the arms of their men, the other hand parading a lavishly decorated mask either suspended on a baton.

Others wore their masks on their faces.

Hors d'oeuvres of the most expensive cheeses, meats and wines decorated tables draped with black silk.

Haunting, classical music played by diligent musicians accompanied the mystifying melody of one of the most well-known sirens of song of the era.

I stood against the wall, arms crossed, wrinkling the black coat which hung over one shoulder, the other hanging over my back.

A black panther mask covered my eyes, white gloves and a crimson scarf finished the ensemble. Balls such as these often bored me but to protect the name of my family, I attended them nonetheless.

The Beauclair clan held one of the most prestigious ranks in our world. Ignoring an invitation to one of their events could be the end of a prosperous dynasty.

I did not know I would be graced by the heiress next in line to the throne of Bertrand Beauclair himself. A cup of wine placed in my hand nearly spilled over her corset as she approached me.

Apologizing profusely for the insult, she assured me all was well.

"I am Catalina Beauclair," she said, her voice a purr. She presented her hand to me, allowing me to kiss it. "You are of the Holloway family? Their last son if I am not mistaken."

I kissed her hand. "Indeed, my lady."

With eyes filled with lust, Catalina invited me to dance with her. Like a fool, I accepted, not knowing how that single moment would impact the rest of my life.

We spun on the floor to countless songs, each one bringing Catalina closer to claiming my mouth in a kiss.

She feigned exhaustion, leading me out of the busy grand ballroom to a hallway overlooking a small garden. The garden reminded me of a place one might go to pray or find solitude to read. I led her to sit, asking if she felt any better.

The kiss came with a hunger – a powerful lust. I pulled back, rising from the stone bench and backing away.

I did not know why my body reacted as it did but if I obeyed such instincts, many nights of pain and loss could have been avoided.

Grace of a serpent did not describe the grace with which Catalina rose from the bench. She strode to me, her gloved hand meeting my chest. "Why did you flee? Was the kiss not to your liking?"

Dizziness overtook the confusion, followed by anger at such a blatant disregard for propriety. Catalina had no knowledge as to if my father deigned me to be married to another woman. Turning my back to her, I told her I needed to leave.

A tender touch on my arm and apologetic eyes were all it took to make me stay.

A weakness that would lead me to a place I never should have gone.

XII. Misuse of Justice

I do not know what time passed by the time I returned home.
Stepping through the doors, I found Walter sitting alone in the den on the lower floor. It irked me to see him in my favorite armchair.

Despite that, after all I went through the night before, arguing or shoving an injured man from my chair did not sit well.

Upon seeing me, Walter attempted to stand only to be told not to move, I would be taking the opposite chair. My hair and clothes stuck to me in lieu of the cold sweat of fatigue beading all over my body.

From the direction of the kitchen, I could smell the scent of Holly's cooking.

Over our years together, she developed many different recipes and how she wanted to open a bakery of her own. "I love to try new things with different recipes I learn from the bakeries in town," she said.

I never complained since they often tasted better than the food prepared by London's finer cafes.

It made me proud to see her wanting to turn her life around.

Holly came into the main room. "Oh!" she gasped when she saw me, quickly returning to the kitchen and making another cup of tea.

When she handed it to me, I reminded her that she did not need to worry herself over me so much. As she did so many times, she shushed me and requested I let her care for me a little.

"Are you okay? You look terrible?" Holly took one of my hands. "You're cold as death. Please tell me you aren't neglecting your needs again."

Smart girl. I smiled a weak smile. "Do not worry, dear one," I said, petting her face. "I will go out tomorrow."

Walter interjected. "I plan on returning to the station to learn what the Inspector has, if anything, regarding this case. I've no inkling of an idea as to what I plan on telling them."

My eyes narrowed. "You must not tell them anything." I rose from the chair, my limbs shaking from exhaustion. "The dawn approaches and I need to rest. Holly, do not leave the grounds alone."

The demanding tone of my words left no room for argument. I retired to my chamber, stripping the wet clothes to the floor.

In the mirror, the cross-shaped scar marring the front of my chest stared back at me. Its memory crept from the confines of my subconscious.

I walked to the bed, allowing my full weight to fall to the silken sheets, my heart aching with pain, anger, rage and a burning vengeance.

* * *

1432

The Night of The Beauclair Fire

Choking smoke tore precious fresh oxygen from my lungs as I skidded across the floor to avoid the elongated nails of the angry woman in front of me. Her fangs glistened in the crimson and orange hues of the flames, the blaze echoing the irateness of the former heiress.

"How could you?" She shrieked, lunging at me, slashing her nails through the air.

I tried to make her calm herself, warning her we needed to get out before the building came crashing down.

She heard none of it, calling me a bastard, a traitor and a whore. None of those labels sat well. I warned her I felt nothing for her. "Please, you must listen to reason, Catalina. This does not need to end in such a manner!"

My words fell on deaf ears.

A marble statue crumbled beneath the weight of a portion of the caving roof. I leapt out of the way, calling Catalina's name, trying to get through the flames. I had little time to move when she flew through the flames, half of her face gone, melted from the heat.

Our nails met in a rain of sparks, clanging together like blades.

"I will never let you go. You are mine. You will always be mine!" She said. Spittle hit me in the face while she spat the possessive words. Her nails found their mark in the middle of my chest.

With my last bit of strength, I shattered Catalina's nails, making her scream. Sadness and pity at how far she fell weighed on my heart.

I kicked her hard enough to send her across the floor into the burning stone. A moan followed by another large portion of the roof caving in ended our battle.

Screams could be heard above the raging flames. Taking the time to get out of the burning mansion, I darted across the yard to avoid any scrutiny.

All of this because I told Catalina nothing would become of the two of us. I dared tell her she could not have what she desired. For my rejection, her home burned.

* * *

The sound of someone pounding on my door, calling my name repeatedly woke me from the nightmare. Sometime during the night I pushed all of the sheets to the side, soaking those beneath me with sweat.

My knuckle hurt, meaning I must have hit the headboard with it again.

Thud. Thud. Thud thud thud. My head began pounding in time with the door.

Holly's voice calling my name made me think she might want to have breakfast again. I got up from the bed, dressed and opened the door to greet Holly, stopping once I saw the tears staining her cheeks.

I did not have the time to ask her what happened. She sobbed into my bare chest, telling me Walter had been arrested upon his arrival at the police station. Sometime during the night, another strange letter appeared on the desk of the secretary in the lobby.

According to Holly, Constable Abrams took Walter for questioning despite the complaints Holly gave him and the alibi she provided in regards to Walter's whereabouts for the past few weeks. I assured Holly I would help the Detective get free of his predicament.

"Wait for me downstairs, I must get dressed." I closed the door, departing to my wardrobe to find suitable attire. The scent of snow lingered on the breeze blowing in through the open window. The soft sounds of the night often helped calm and relax me into a state so I could sleep so I tended to sleep with the curtains drawn, windows open.

I met Holly at the foot of the stairs where she begged me to let her come with me. In light of Catalina's re-emergence, I ordered Holly to stay at the mansion where I knew she would remain safe, opened the double doors and vanished into mist.

* * *

Being amongst the populace tended to rattle me despite being in the form of a stray black cat or dog often seen on the busy streets and alleys. The populace would overlook me at times, kick or curse at me others. It never bothered me since it did not hinder me from getting where I needed to go.

With a grunt, I leapt from the cold cement to the rickety old fence separating the police station from the abandoned lot. Snow stuck to my black fur, agitating me, making me shiver against the chill.

Shifting to the rat, I ascended the black wiring connected to a rusted vent capable of allowing fresh air to flow in and out of the building. My claws clacked across the brick, not loud enough to draw any attention but enough to bother my sensitive hearing.

It took me a few attempts until I heard Walter's voice almost yelling at whomever interrogated him.

From the sounds of it, the person had to be the beautiful Sergeant Penelope Thompson.

A slight grin curled across my large incisors. If Penelope and Walter were the only ones in the room, setting him free would be easier than I thought.

Perfect. I thought, not wanting to have to hit an unsuspecting man since the irate feelings of the night before still lingered.

I watched through the grate while Penelope sighed. She crossed her arms over her impressive breasts. "Walter, I like you, okay? All I want to know is where you've been the last few weeks. You reported you were with your lover but not where you were. Seems suspicious."

Walter averted his eyes.

In truth, it would not have mattered if he did choose to speak despite my warning the night before. No one would believe him and think him a madman, locking him up as I had seen happen to so many others. It is one reason I chose to leave those I fed on with thoughts posing as dreams.

Penelope heaved a sigh. With her thumb and forefingers, she rubbed the bridge of her nose.

I used the opportunity to descend into the shadows, shifting into my human form.

Walter saw me, wide-eyed but kept quiet when I held a finger over my mouth.

My hand took Penelope's hip, scaring her. She spun around, swinging a fist at me which I caught and sensually lowered. Smiling, I worked my charms on her, stripping her of any control and talking her into handing me the keys to Walter's shackles. Musing, she handed me the keys. I kissed her lips, turning so my back faced Walter, handing him the keys.

"Unlock yourself," I said, returning my attention to Penelope. Starving, I lost any care as to who remained in the room.

I let my fangs caress Penelope's neck, her blood calling out to be drawn from her veins.

"Stop!" Walter called out in a hushed voice.

It frustrated me to be interrupted. I had not fed properly in so long. However, Walter had worked with this woman and did not know the extent of the world he stepped into.

With an agitated "Very well," I left Penelope with her dream, took the form of the black mist, wrapped around Walter and took us both out through the vents.

Landing in the alley, I fought back a wave of dizziness. Changing shape cost a large quantity of energy. To move another cost two times the regular amount. Taking some clothes off a clothesline, I told Walter to change and discard his.

Shuffling officers and the sounds of multiple whistles filled the enclosed space.

I pushed Walter down the back way, keeping to the shadows as best we could. When we finally reached the edge of the woods, all of London became an uproar of officers looking for their "escaped prisoner."

Sweat trickled down my cheeks to my collar. I needed to feed soon or the energy required to do what needed to be done would take too long to obtain.

The journey back to Raven Hollow remained silent, my frustration filling the air so thick, I knew Walter could feel it.

Outside the brick walls surrounding the mansion, Walter stopped me. "I'm sorry. I don't know what happened. I know-"

"You know nothing." My fist slammed into the brick, fracturing the vine covered stone. "Had you been intelligent, you would have listened to me when I told you to remain at Raven Hollow. This is not a case you can solve using mortal methods."

Walter stood silent. At his side, his hands rolled into fists, jaw tight into a thin line, eyes squeezed shut.

I could hear his teeth grinding behind his lips, his heart racing in his chest. I knew he wanted to say something. I gave him no opening to do so.

Finishing my rant, I sighed. "Listen to me, stay in Raven Hollow for now. I do not expect you to understand, no mortal does. What I will say is you and Holly are in terrible danger. Our enemy is powerful, cunning and willing to do anything she can."

Confusion filled eyes met mine.

I shook my head, asking him to leave things alone and promising I would do whatever I could to make sure neither he nor Holly would be hurt.

Deep inside, I knew the only way to protect them would be to send them away. Something that tore at my heart worse than anything Catalina could do.

XIII. Wanted

Holly paced the floor of the foyer when Walter and I walked through the large double doors. My daughter ran to the man she confessed to love, holding him close to her, smiling and crying.

Mouthing "thank you," the two of them stayed in the foyer kissing and hugging one another. The scene made me smile, yet sad at what I knew needed to be done. Catalina's relentless nature forced me to do something drastic in order to keep Walter and Holly safe.

Holly parted from Walter, making her way over to me and placing a warm hand on my cheek. A light gasp escaped her. "Jonathan."

I silenced her. "I am fine, dearest. I will go out later, I promise."

The answer seemed to placate the small woman. She returned to her lover, her fingers entwined with his.

It reminded me of all the times she did the same with me, promising she would marry me when she came of age.

This must be what being a parent feels like. Memories of Holly as a little girl confronted me, reminding me of how all we went through was indeed worth it.

Notes went out with the groundskeeper, promising him I would pay him extra to make sure I heard back from the letters I sent in a timely manner.

True to his word, the man returned with the documentation I requested and a small decorated box covered in ornate butterflies, baring my family crest.

At dinner, my heart pounded with the knowledge Holly would fight me to stay by my side.

For most of the gathering I remained silent, trying to find the perfect words to say, knowing all too well such words did not exist. I had saved Holly and Walter's life. Both of them would want to do what they could to help me, I remained certain.

With the fortitude gathered, I called attention from everyone at the table. "I want the two of you to leave for Nottingham within the next two days."

As I predicted, Holly's rebuttal came swiftly. "Why on Earth would you say that?"

Walter kept his intense eyes glaring at me while I leaned forward, intertwining my fingers, propping myself against them. "Holly, there is no more you can do for me. It is the only way the two of you can live a life together. I have already made all of the arrangements. You will have the money and a home to raise a family."

The two of them gasped, eyes bulging in disbelief. The rest of the meal passed in silence yet tense.

Walter pulled me aside after dinner, his cheeks a burning red. Something unbecoming of an English gentleman of his usually strong stature. Twiddling his thumbs and the aversion of his eyes indicated to me what I already believed coming.

When he finally spoke, his voice came out in a whisper. "I wanted to request your permission to marry Holly, sir. I planned on asking her tonight in the garden next to the fountain. It's her favorite place, you see -"

Walter rambled anything he seemed to think of to persuade me to allow him to marry my beloved daughter.

In reply to his prattling, I asked him a single question, wanting to know if he promised to protect her. His counter to my words came in the form of an irrefutable "Yes, I swear."

I saw no lie in his eyes, thinking about his willingness to face the ghoul. "Very well. Take care of her, Mr. Deverough. I will hunt you down and kill you should she ever call on me and tell me you broke your word."

My words cut deep enough I saw the slightest tremble in Walter's body. From experience, I knew mortal fathers were hard to ask to court their daughters. My being an immortal father capable of many things more than doubled the risk.

Walter thanked me and all but skipped off like a child in a schoolyard playing hop-scotch. I smiled and departed to my study to be stopped by Holly, curious if she heard any of the conversation.

Tears pooled at the corners of her eyes, causing her facial makeup to begin to run. Such an acute glare would petrify any man into wondering what they had done to earn it. Knowing Holly, I did not need to ask such a question.

"I know what you are going to say, dearest heart, but I am not going to discuss it further," I replied.

What came next, I did not expect. Holly hugged me tightly, her cheek settled against my chest. Informing me she knew of Walter's intent to propose, she asked if I would help her plan the wedding by spending the following day with her. "I want my father to help me pick out a dress and talk to the Church. Please do this for me. I will miss you so."

In such a short sentence, my heart lurched into my throat. A hard lump threatened to hinder my ability to breath. As I planned the couple's escape to safety, it never occurred to me I might not ever get to see the wedding. I might not get to see my grandchildren.

Closing my eyes, I placed a soft kiss on Holly's hair, taking her in my own firm hug. "Yes. It would be your father's honor."

* * *

Later that night, I stood hidden in the form of a raven in a tree stripped of its leaves by winter's bitterness. Anna paced at the bottom of the trunk, glancing up at me with an eager glance.

Walter sat on the edge of the fountain with Holly, the two of them silent.

Would it not give me away, I would have guffawed at such a dramatic scene. It never made sense to me how mortals made such a fuss over telling one how fond they were of them.

Eventually, Walter took the black box I gave him following my talk with Holly.

A family heirloom – a ring belonging to my mother – resided in a soft bed of velvet. Genuine onyx lay in the finest gold since silver tended to burn us. If ever I chose to sell it, the amount I would receive rivaled that of one of the king's jewels.

Despite her knowing about the proposal, Holly screamed in happiness when Walter asked her to marry him. She threw herself at him, knocking them both from the fountain to the snow on the ground.

Thank goodness for the new fallen snow. I thought, laughing to myself.

I looked down at Anna, nodding.

A smile lit across her face and she pranced across the garden.

For as long as Holly had been at Raven Hollow, Anna put herself in the role of the spectral mother. Holly never knew she resided in the garden, but Anna told me many times how she played with Holly without her ever seeing Anna.

My memories slipped back to the days when my daughter came into my life. With the widest of grins, I allowed them to play like a series of photos in my mind.

To know Holly lived such a life in a place avoided by the populace made me proud. I had worried that she would live in constant terror while in fact, she befriended many of the childrens' spirits.

I waited for Walter and Holly to depart before dropping to the ground beneath the shadow of the fountain. Anna joined me, her chilled, yet gentle hands encasing my feathered body, raising me into her lap.

I found if I allowed one of my shapes to keep a certain aspect of mist, Anna could touch me, almost as if she were alive.

I will miss her. The words came out as a muted cry of a carrion bird.

XIV. Holly

I lied to you before. Hell arrived for me much earlier as you can probably tell from the memories I recorded within these pages. I see no reason to repeat what has already been said.

Holly tugged at my arm towards one of the local shops containing a seamstress who pieced together some of the most beautiful dresses London had ever seen.

Try as I might, her cheerful tone and light smile did nothing to lift the sorrowful spirit plaguing me from the night before. Anna had stroked my feathered body, doing what she could to calm me.

Determination kept me from displaying any of these melancholy emotions to Holly due to our outing being the last I would have with my daughter. I smiled when she pointed to the shop, allowing her to pull me across the street. I nearly lost the hat I wore to the gusts of snow-mixed wind at the force of her tug on my hand.

The door above our heads tinkled with the sound of a small bell suspended by a thin silver wire resembling something one might find in a master's mansion for his servants. I knew them since sections of Raven Hollow's rooms contained the same bells.

A portly woman with a large feathered hat and double-chin greeted us when we walked in. Her cheerful disposition added to Holly's jovial mood when the two began chattering about wedding gowns and what colors the bride and groom chose.

I never understood why women made such a ruckus over their color choices. Though I suppose I would not since I never married myself.

"This is my father," Holly said to the woman, taking my arm.

Smiling a broad smile, the woman winked at me, her eyes taking in every detail of my body and face despite my attempts to keep my immortal allure in check.

Another reason why I prefer seclusion. I sighed, my shoulders dropping, eyes rolling at the woman who introduced herself as Lillian.

While the two jabbered, I took the opportunity to slink away and walk through the confines of the shop. My mind imagined what many of the dresses would look like if I ever got the chance to see Anna in them.

Moving on, I found many different types of jewelry ranging from earrings, rings, bracelets and necklaces. They all looked quite stunning and expensive.

One of the trinkets, a necklace in a glass case, captured my eye.

At the end of a ribbon, a heart garnished with ruby glistened in the muted light of the day. Its beauty both captivated and entranced me. Thoughts of the crimson life force I desperately needed made the end of my fangs burn.

No. Not now. To keep control I drew upon the nightmares of Anna, of Walter, of the mangled bodies – anything to push the need away long enough for me to dote on Holly.

Holly. I glanced over to where Holly and the woman still prattled. Holly wore a silken white dress, gloves and a veil.

I smiled with pride, thinking back to the day I first met her and when she came to Raven Hollow.

* * *

The little mud coated urchin glared at me beneath her filthy hair. Had she been able to, I had no doubt she would have set me ablaze with those fiery blue eyes laced with clear disdain.

I had no idea why I chose to save her from the police, chose to load her into my carriage and spirit her away to a haunted mansion in a secluded forest on an English hillside. I questioned myself the whole way, wondering if I could still take her back to the police

She sat across from me, staring at me, her muddy cheeks red with blush.

"What is your name, little one?" I asked, trying to deter her from her hateful glare.

Scoffing, she folded her small arms tighter across her chest, refusing to answer.

Being the gentleman, I repeated my question.

The reply came out more biting than I initially imagined. "Why do you bloody care? You, who obviously has money, all dressed in your high class knickers and satin ascot."

I chuckled behind closed lips. "I believe your use of the term knickers is a bit flawed."

Silence resumed between us until the driver informed me we had arrived at our destination.

As with many of those brave enough to ferry me to the edge of the woods, I paid the driver well, thanking him for the ride. He promised me he remained in my service despite never going to my home.

It mattered little to me. I preferred walking through the forest, hearing the howling wolves and calling of the owls and ravens.

With the girl, however, the walk would remain anything but silent. Her questions flooded my ears, starting with who would want to live in such a foul place.

Things only grew worse when we came to Raven Hollow.

"Bloody hell," she said. "Who could live in such a wicked place as this?"

I never imagined such language coming from a young girl but learning where she grew up, all mystery faded away as to why she held such a decorative vocabulary.

"This is my home."

My reply brought about a laugh and a request to "quit jesting" to which I glared at her, ending the conversation.

* * *

"What do you think?" Holly's words broke through my memories, bringing me back to the present.

"What? My apologies, love, will you kindly repeat what you said?" I requested. She did, spinning around to make the dress twirl and flow around her. "It is indeed beautiful. I remember the first time I asked you to wear a dress for me."

Holly huffed through her lips, making her sound like a horse. "You wanted to send me to boarding school to learn how to be a lady."

"Indeed." I laughed. She'd been adamant on that day to stay home, her blue-grey eyes full of defiance.

When the carriage arrived to take her away, she managed to hide herself so well not even I could find her for hours.

Eventually, I managed to force her into the pastel pink dress and bonnet earning a look, again, that could set me aflame if she possessed such a power.

To say this petite woman brought great adventure into my life would be an understatement. Everything I tried to teach her often ended in a fight until she figured out how to do things on her own.

Seeing her, excited about marriage and choosing the correct earrings to wear with her dress and veil,made the days of her childhood seem so long ago.

The rising of the hairs on the back of my neck and the familiar scent made me leap quickly, shouting for Holly to move out of the way just as the ghoul broke through the glass.

Quickly using my body, I shielded both Holly and my head from the shattering glass and crumbling ceiling.

Screams echoed all around us as the patrons tried to understand what just happened. I shook the shards from my hair, taking in Holly's condition. "Are you hurt, dear one?"

The scent of blood wafted through the air. It caused the raging burn in my fangs to go awry, threatening my sense of control.

Across the room, I could make out the shape of a man sitting on his haunches.

The sickening slurping of a ravaging ghoul trying to satiate its hunger invaded my sensitive ears. It uttered he muted words as it tore into the body of the shop owner who helped Holly choose her dress.

"Feed...so...hungry," The thing slurped the soft innards.

Beneath me, I felt Holly start to rise. I wrapped my body around her in a protective hug.

"No. Do not look. Please, I beg you." My eyes closed tight. I uttered a silent prayer that Holly did not see the gory details; that she had not seen the monster in the shape of a man.

Once the ghoul finished ravaging the woman, it turned to look over its shoulder. The scraggly, wiry beard oozed with crimson gore and fluids, the ivory remnants of teeth and sunken eyes curling up in a smile.

It rose from its haunches. Distorted, elongated limbs dangled and twitched at its side.

All of the patrons elected to leave in light of seeing how many bodies the ghoul managed to mangle in a short amount of time. Their departure made it easier for me to stand against the lowly beast.

I rose from the floor, turning my body towards the ghoul, keeping Holly shielded as best I could from the carnage. "Dearest, I need you to go. Now."

Holly stuttered behind me. Her trembling hand clenching my black jacket made my heart lurch with pain and anger.

This creature dared to kill on my territory, not once but many times. It terrified my daughter and ruined an important event in her life.

"F-father," Holly said behind me.

I knew the risks of what I did but I lacked the care. My daughter needed me.

I turned to take her small shoulders in my hands. "Listen to me. Look only at me. You need to leave. Go home to Walter and the two of you pack. I will be home soon. You have your father's word."

I knew her well, the fight in her eyes willing her to defy me. "Holly, this is not up for debate. I will distract it."

Tears welled up in Holly's eyes as she turned to leave.

I stopped her, handing her the dress, petting her face and making her promise not to let what happened ruin our day together.

The smile I received added to the anger I intended to use on the ghoul.

When I knew Holly was out of harm's way, I turned my attention back to the ghoul. I could feel the heat that accompanied my eyes when they changed into the eyes of a cat and glowed rings of silver.

Stalking forward like the predator inside of me, my nails extended into thick blades. "You dare attack one of your betters, lowest of the low. At your mistresses' behest or not, you have the gall to threaten my daughter, kill in my home. I will see you writhing at my feet as you plead for your wretched life!"

A wicked grin in a mouth full of jagged teeth chuckled back at me. It said something but I understood none of it due to how far along the mutation had gotten.

Screaming it lunged at me, missing, careening into the mirrors of the dressing room. I glided across the floor, aware of the dizzying effects of the blood all over the room.

I must leave this place, I thought, stepping back, bending my body out of the way of the ghoul's blood-covered hands.

Such a simple movement should not have taken so much out of me but my lack of feeding and fatigue wore on me. I had to get the ghoul to follow me to a place I could tear its throat out without too many mortals figuring out what went on.

Another primal screech erupted from the ghoul as it emerged from the shattered glass.

Taking the opportunity, I whipped around, shifting into the form of the Great Dane and barking at the monster.

Seeing me, it frantically dug its claws into the flooring, nails emitting a shrill noise trying to get hold but to no avail.

I ran as fast as I could, shifting to mist and back to the hound through the busy streets.

Behind me, the ghoul kept the form of the starved man, shoving people aside, the action slowing it. I grinned, thankful to have been able to buy myself some much needed time.

XV. Hunted

Once again, I stood face to face with the ghoul responsible for attacking my daughter not once but twice. Rage heated the blood in my body, my heart pounding as I pushed the canine form I had taken to its limits.

Behind me the ghoul screamed, his leather boots crunching the dead foliage on the forest floor. Trying to trick it out of the city seemed to take hours. Onlookers stopped, trying to find out what the commotion was about.

No doubt our presence alerted the local authorities who swarmed the dress shop after we left, questioning witnesses.

Those affected by the ruckus on the street where the ghoul shoved them aside in pursuit of a black dog probably looked as shocked as those in the shop.

I managed to get Holly to safety while still managing to get her the dress she grew fond of. Due to the shop owner's untimely and grisly demise, I doubted the police cared about a missing item of clothing or two.

I shifted back into the form of a man, watching the ghoul panting.

Blood dripped from its mouth along with small chunks of gore.

A distended belly, from gorging on bodies, poked out from beneath its tattered shirt. To the average Englishman on the street, this man would appear to be nothing more than a hobo.

My eyes furrowed with rage at the smile crawling across its face. Something sounding like a raspy, gnarled laugh came from the back of its throat.

In mere moments, the ghoul lunged at me screaming "feed" at the top of its lungs.

I side-stepped it, hitting it with the side of my hand. My nails extended into the blades from the shop, my fangs growing past my mouth's ability to contain them. The eyes of the cat replaced those of the man, turning to radiant silver.

Even in a weakened state, the madness of the parasite in the ghoul's brain, planted there by his mistress, had taken over all rational thought.

Time and again, the ghoul lunged, missing me with every turn.

The fight became more a twisted dance of survival on the ghoul's part rather than mine.

Despite my changed nature since meeting Anna, I found myself relishing the thing's helplessness. I could kill it at any point; tear its guts from its taut skin and feel the blood on my nails as I did in my bygone past.

No! I shook my head, allowing the ghoul the opening it needed to rake its own nails across my side, tearing into the fabric of my shirt into the flesh underneath. I cried out, regaining my focus and moving quickly to wrap my forearm around the creature's throat.

"You," I growled through clenched teeth, raising my nails. "Will never," I slammed the blades through the ghoul's mid-section. "Ever hurt my daughter or the man she loves again."

The ghoul writhed and howled in pain as I continued to plunge my nails through its ashen skin.

Gore and blood coated my hand up to my wrist. It filled me with a sense of ecstasy at feeling the pull and push of flesh, the hunter in me elated to feel the rush and smell of death again.

By the time I finished, the ghoul fell limp on my arm, suspended in the air by my strength. I dropped the corpse to my feet, looking at both of my hands, my chest heaving.

Falling to my knees in the gore, I screamed, angry at myself for feeling the way I did, furious I let my self-control go to fulfill an evil nature I long thought I locked away.

My side ached from the place where the ghoul impaled me. It did not mask the shame I felt.

Holly. I have to go see Holly. She and Walter would leave soon to Nottingham – away from all of this.

One thing remained before I could go home. The fight took more out of me than I thought and I needed to feed.

* * *

By the time I got home, Holly paced back and forth beside the carriage waiting to take her and Walter away. I could hear the detective telling her they needed to go before it became too dark. She, in return, refused to go anywhere until I returned.

A father could not have displayed a brighter smile at his daughter's words.

When she noticed me, Holly ran up to me. "Thank God!" She hugged me, earning one in return.

Holly backed away, her eyes looking at me, taking in my condition from my feet to my head. Her eyes grew sullen. "You fed."

I closed my eyes, nodding.

"Fatal?" She asked.

Again, I nodded. "Forgive me, dear one. I had no choice."

Shaking her head, Holly took me in another hug, claiming she did not care as long as I remained okay.

The man I fed upon showed such concern when I collapsed under a tree in the local park. He asked if I needed to go to a hospital, which I politely declined by asking him to forgive me and sank my fangs in his throat.

During the attack, he gagged, begging me to stop, stating he had a wife and children. I could not stop the guilt from swallowing my soul but still I kept feeding until he fell limp in my dark embrace.

I am a monster wearing the face of a man. The words echoed in my mind as I stared above the young man's lifeless body, my wounds healing, my strength returning.

Walter called out to Holly from the carriage. I took her shoulders in my hands, begging her to leave, promising she would have a chance at a life away from the darkness. She could raise a family away from the monsters, the angry ghosts and superstition.

Pulling me down, she whispered. "I love you, father. I will always love you."

I kissed her hair, tears pooling in the corners of my eyes. "And I you, my dearest. Go. Please."

As late afternoon turned to evening, I stood in the growing shadows watching them disappear down the road. The tears I held back to avoid making the separation worse when Holly stood before me broke free, streaming down my face.

My only comfort remained in the knowledge she would be safe from the battle yet to come. *Everything will end in the next few days.*

* * *

With Holly and Walter gone, I found remaining at Raven Hollow difficult due to loneliness and melancholy.

I departed back to the streets of London, taking the rare walk amongst the people who once called my daughter a witch. The same people who condemned my beloved home as a house of evil spirits and vengeful ghosts babbled gossip about the events earlier that afternoon.

Police wandered the streets en masse. Abrams stood on the street corner leading to the docks talking to the same officer who dismissed the young officer who questioned the existence of blood-sucking immortals.

I focused on what they said.

Abrams mentioned the murder in the park of the good samaritan who gave his life so I could regain some strength.

This will never end. I reminded myself. *She will kill here until I am either forced to move or kill to survive.*

Every event starting from the first murder came to the forefront of my thoughts. Drawing on the furiousness I exhibited during my fight with the ghoul, I began hunting.

I will find you Catalina. This time, I will make sure you die. My inhuman speed made the passers-by believe they experienced a strong gust of wind, the women gasping when their skirts were caught.

The scent of Catalina on the ghoul would lead me to where she hid – the docks of London.

XV. Dead Man's Blood

Why in the name of the night would Catalina be here? I questioned, standing on the edge of the docks. The same place I tracked the ghoul to the first time - a covered cobblestone fish market and loading dock - lay before me.

In all the years I knew Catalina, never once did I find myself seeing her in such a rundown area.

During the day, the fish market bustled with activity but at night, it became an eerie sight. Abandoned dock houses were strewn along the harbor and bay area. *The perfect place for one of my kind to hide.*

Inhaling a deep breath, I caught a faint scent on the air. Catalina's perfume mixed with the smell of rotten fish guts and decaying carcasses. The latter resembled the same scent as the ghoul I killed.

Something didn't feel right.

The scents appeared old but for a brief moment, I could smell something fresh. *What is going on?*

Keeping to the shadows, I followed the scents to the very end of the docks where a crumbling boathouse, its doors chained together with rusted chains, stood isolated.

According to local legend, a band of privateers used it to smuggle the first batch of goods onto a ship waiting out in the harbor. They were caught and eventually executed by being drowned in the harbor by an anchor chain strapped to their boots.

Since then, anyone who ventured too close reported hearing clattering chains and the haunting shanty of a cursed pirate at sea.

The entire section of the dock remained cut off from the bustling market.

If Catalina's intent was to remain hidden, she found the ideal spot. I could not stop myself from wondering what else she might be up to.

The nauseating smell of rot gave away the presence of the ghouls behind me. I turned to see not only one but three of them glaring back at me. From their physical states I could tell they had only begun their descent into insanity.

Something seemed strange, they did not attack. Their tongues fell from their mouths, drool cascading down their chins to their clothes. One of them licked the saliva, begging to feed.

I prepared for it to attack only to receive the sharp sting of a blade in my side. Accompanying the blade, a frozen flame flooding through my veins like shards of glass had been injected into me.

"Dead man's.." I said with a wheeze.

Slender, feminine fingers wound about my throat, caressing it, tracing over my Adam's apple, up my jaw.

"Hello, Jonathan, so glad to see you again." Catalina's voice purred in my ear.

Withdrawing the blade, Catalina thrust it into my back, the same sensation as before erupting anew in my veins.

Dead man's blood. One of the only substances capable of either rendering my kind weak enough to capture or keep imprisoned, invaded my body, rending my veins and causing my heart to stall for seconds at a time.

During the time of the Plague, the Church hired hunters capable of using the vile fluid to kill us and present our severed heads to the priests for coin. Even those higher in the caste struggled against its effects if given enough.

My body hit the frigid, wet stink of the cobblestone, weak and growing weaker.

Catalina stood above me fiddling with the knife blade while I gripped the wound in my side. "This pains me more than you could ever know. You could have been beside me and ruled with the same strength you once held."

I found myself chuckling at how deep her delusion blinded her. As often as I denied her, swore to her I would rather die, she thought she could own me, force me to become her consort.

Once I learned she belonged to one of the most powerful counts during the reign of the Scots, I quickly made sure she and I would never be.

It drove Catalina mad. She knelt beside me, gripped my hair and pulled until our eyes met. "You have no power anymore, Holloway. Your downfall began the moment you scorned my advances. What gives you the right to chortle at me?"

"Nothing except how arrogant you are. I told you then, I will tell you now. I will never be yours. Never will I warm your bed or help you murder the count."

My reply enraged Catalina further. Using her immortal strength, she threw my head against the cobblestone, blurring my vision.

Through the fog of my brain, I heard Catalina command one of her ghouls to take me prisoner. With the poison in my veins, I had few options.

As hard as I could, I kicked the ghoul's legs out from under it, hauled myself to my feet and plunged into the hypothermic water of the harbor.

The moment I hit in the icy darkness, my breath drained from my lungs. Voices from above became muffled in the void.

I opened my eyes, clenched my teeth and utilized what adrenaline I could find to propel through the water, barely avoiding a net being thrown in.

With luck, I could make it to the far side of the river, temporarily out of the grasp of Catalina and her ghouls.

I had no inkling as to how much time passed when I finally emerged from the water to get a much needed breath for my aching lungs.

My side throbbed, blood full of what felt like daggers in my veins. Every attempt I made to take the slightest breath became harder as I hauled myself onto the pier.

Which one, I did not know.

In the end, my strength gave out and I fell back into the water, sinking into blackness. *It is just as well. I have many sins to atone for.*

* * *

When next I woke I stared at the wooden ceiling of what looked like a shack. From the scent, I could only assume it to belong to a fisherman. Nets, boat tackle, ropes and blades dangled from suspensions attached to the ceiling and walls.

Surveying the condition of my body, I saw that my jacket and shirt had been removed.

The wounds in my side and lower back had been cleaned and wrapped with gauze wrappings. I remembered nothing after slipping from the pier except the brief image of what I imagined to be a fever dream.

Thin rope wrapped around my body, entangling in the buttons and cusps of my jacket and limbs.

I tried to struggle but the toxin inside me halted any effort I might have made. Soon I found my body hauled from the water onto a hard surface.

For mere seconds, I opened my eyes to see the shadow of a man standing above me. I surrendered to the idea it might be a ghoul, believing I would be on my way back to Catalina.

By whatever grace the saints found to give a monster like me, I escaped the clutches of death or at worst, enslavement.

The dark thoughts were pushed to the back of my mind so I could find out where I was. It took a strong resolution to defy my body's desire to remain in the make-shift bed. *I survived the encounter, barely. What happens when my luck runs out?*

"You're awake. Good." A gruff, baritone voice broke through my thoughts.

In the door walked a gentleman relying on a cane to support a rather bothersome limp in his right leg.

Upon his face, a long beard and pseudo-handlebar mustache hid a multitude of scars. He wore an eye patch over his left eye while the other sported a nasty set of scars.

Were I a betting man, I would assume he came across some rough company in his life.

A wooden bench creaked as he sat upon it, lighting a thick cigar, inhaling only to let out an awful cough. "There was a moment, I didn't think you would wake up."

XVI. Hunter

The strange gentleman sat in silence, staring at the fire in the rickety old black stove, its maw radiating a faded glow of reds and oranges.

Behind its grate, I could see the wood charring to a black as dark as the stove itself. I had seen many like it but still, it held an almost hypnotic effect.

Knowing I could not linger long enough to let my wounds heal, I addressed my host. "I want to thank you, sir, for saving me but I must be going."

My host took out a pipe and proceeded to light it. As he puffed on the end, he stared into the flames of the stove, his mind seeming to drift.

"I know what you are," The gentleman said through the silence. He took another puff off the pipe, exhaling the smoke before continuing. "I know what poison flows through your veins."

Who is this man? I wondered. If he knew what I truly was then he must have come across one of my kin. "Forgive me but I do not believe you know what I am. Now, I must insist you -"

The man cut me off, standing from his seat.

Flames from the stove flickered cinders in his eyes.

I knew not if what I saw happened to be anger or insult at what I said. "I do know. A monster wearing the face of a man. A creature who drinks the life of man or leads young women astray to feed on their sexual pleasure. Do you truly not remember me?"

I could feel the changing of my eyes in the presence of the man I realized to be a hunter - a mortal with skills and abilities to stand against the beings of the night. "I see. So you are a slave of the Church. Why did you not kill me when you had the chance?"

The hunter turned his back – a dangerous, often fatal thing to do – when faced with one of us. "You spared my life once. You showed me not all monsters are wicked. I would know you even if both of my eyes were blind."

Still, despite his words, I could not place the man's face. *I spared him?* My brow raised, puzzled.

A gruff laugh bellowed, ending with a slight cough. "My name is Leland Kietch. I was sent to dispatch you in Spain while you visited the monarchs. Of course," He gestured to his leg. "I didn't have this to contend with at the time."

I could feel the man's pain.

My sensitivities to the heart, blood and lungs indicated Leland was not long for this world. In a few months time, he would be dead.

It saddened me to see when realization and memory brought back familiar images.

A strong young hunter had gone toe to toe with me at my most ruthless stage in life. For the first time, I believed I had found the man capable of killing me. For only a man can kill a monster.

I sighed. "I do remember you. Time has not been kind, old friend."

The use of the word "friend" probably indicated a bond. What we had between us was respect between rivals.

Leland hunted me for years then suddenly stopped. Long I believed him to be dead.

Leland sat back down, thrown into a coughing fit.

I offered him some water despite knowing it would not help him.

He waved it off, leaning back against the wall. His tattered coat fell over the bench to the dusty floor.

"Why did you not seek me out? Did you know I resided here?" I asked.

Leland nodded. "I knew. Like you, I suppose I wanted to remain hidden, live the quiet life of a fisherman since I could no longer carry a blade or holy weapon. I also knew what was going on here. Unfortunately, my body lacked the strength to do what my heart wanted."

It hurt to sit down on the bench opposite Leland. Dizziness and nausea from the dead man's blood threatened to empty my stomach of its contents.

"Dead man's blood. Never ceases to have one hell of an effect," Leland tried to chuckle. "Listen, I know you can see I'm not going to be around much longer. If the beast who did that to you is the one killing people, I want to do what I can. Take one more abomination down before being sent to Hell."

I lowered my gaze to the floor, the silver lined gaze boring a hole into the floor, hands clasped between spread legs. "You cannot know what you ask, Leland. I do not kill needlessly nor would I do so to a man who deserves a more worthy death."

Leland informed me of how I would be doing him a favor. He had been to doctors who said he would only grow worse, suffering a deteriorating condition, his body devouring itself from the inside.

As much agony as it brought me to learn, I could not push the memories away long enough to believe such a horrifying fate awaiting him.

* * *

Barcelona, Spain

I stepped out of the carriage onto the streets of beautiful Barcelona, Spain. The clear night a grand stage for the full moon died the color of blood. The Hunter's moon stared back at me, her light bathing me in glorious radiance. It mattered little why I had been invited to stand in the presence of the ruling monarch if I could see such a beautiful city.

Almost immediately, I could sense something did not seem right. All around me, patrons stared as if they had not expected me to come.

One of them, a young woman met me and curtsied. "My Lord, welcome. I have been instructed to lead you to the gardens where the princess awaits you. If you would be so kind."

It annoyed me but I followed the woman, whom I gathered to be a servant, to the garden only to be ambushed by a hunter.

The fire in the man's eyes excited me, his determination separating him from so many others who tried to end my life only to fall by my hand.

Our battle resembled more of an elegant dance than an attempt at bloodshed.

I laughed, addressing my opponent. "Tell me your name, young hunter. I must know whom I am to praise for such a glorious battle."

He told me, huffing under his breath then lunging at me with a sword brandished with the crest of the Catholic church. Young Leland showed more promise than any man I stood against in my years of life.

The longer our battle continued, the wider the smile on my face grew.

A ghoul's appearance disrupted the fight, infuriating me. I wanted so much more from my dear hunter.

It shocked me to see the ghoul turned its attention to Leland. A shriek followed by a cry of pain echoed in the emptiness. Had this been an act to end both of our lives?

Beyond the body of the ghoul, I saw Leland struggling to hold it back, sword wedged between its incisors. If I did not act, the young man would die, a promising rival taken from this world.

Leaping into the air, I plunged my elongated nails through the monster's back, tearing its spine from it and throwing the body aside like rubbish.

Leland panted beneath me, his eyes holding the remnants of defiance.

I smiled, offered my hand to help pull him to his feet.

Leland shoved my hand away, relying on his own strength to stand. "Why did you help me?"

I could see a mortal wound in his shoulder. "You hold promise, young hunter. Our fight is over for now but seek me out when you have healed. It has been many years since I have met someone with a will of iron. Perhaps we will meet again soon."

* * *

"...need to do this."

I shook my head, returning to the present, not knowing when I drifted into the vault of my memories. Leland had been speaking but I did not hear any of it.

"Apologies, would you mind repeating yourself?" I asked.

He did, telling me that he needed to do something to help against Catalina. The pride of a hunter would forbid him from having an honorable death unless he did something to avenge all of the innocents who died. "It would be payment in return for your sparing my life."

No doubt remained inside of me as to what I needed to do in order to stand against Catalina.

In my current state, I barely had a chance against her, let alone her ghouls.

Still, the thought of taking Leland's blood until he died sat ill with me. I would have wanted to allow him the chance to die in battle had his injury to his leg not been so severe.

Again, I denied him, taking my shirt and jacket from the nearby closet where I spotted them during our talk. Blood stains and holes where the knife pierced my side stared back at me.

"Can't fight in those," Leland said.

Rising from his chair, he limped into the small space I took to be his sleeping quarters, returning with a change of clothes similar to what he wore. "Use these. They don't really resemble anything a noble would wear but they'll do."

I changed quickly, readying myself for whatever I might face when I saw Catalina again.

When I came out, Leland glared at me. It did not take an awareness higher than a mortal to see what he thought. "I've seen that girl of yours. Why did you take her in? Raise her as your own?"

The small wooden door creaked an awful whine when I opened it. Speaking over my shoulder, I said, "I never claimed to be a good man but not all monsters are the same. I would think you above all people would know this by now."

I left him with my final words, feeling the smile at my back.

XVII. Rest In Peace, Dear Friend

The journey back to Raven Hollow Manor proved to be more difficult than I thought. Sweat dripped down my brows onto the raised collar of the chocolate brown coat which dangled down passed my knees. Against the fog and the cold weather, the coat did well to shield me but it seemed heavier.

A strong smell of smoke drifted on the night air.

No! I thought, beginning to sprint.

Billows of smoke appeared above the trees, their fumes forming a dark cloud riding the wind towards London.

Across the ground, the fog grew thicker from the heat of the flames and the chill of the snow and wind.

I arrived at the brick wall, the iron gate lay strewn across the ground.

I thought of Anna - how scared she must be, wondering where I was. I thought of the demon beneath the mansion, praying no one had opened its coffin, releasing it upon the unsuspecting city.

Overwhelming grief niggled at my heart when I came to the house. Its infrastructure had been engulfed in raging flames, the wood whining as it tried to stand against the roaring fire.

My...my home. I could not believe the sight.

All of the years I spent with Holly, all of the effort I put into remaining hidden in plain sight all burned before my eyes, ripping into my heart, making me forget the poison ravaging my body.

Hitting the ground, I cried out to the heavens, tears of blood streaming from eyes squeezed shut. I had only myself to blame for the sins leading me to this point.

The whining of the wood sounded like cries of pain and agony as the mansion started to buckle under the inferno. Precious work put into tending the gardens had come to naught. Cries of the spirits within begged to be set free so they did not burn in the flames.

Annabelle knelt beside me, holding me and mouthing she could not stay much longer. When I asked why, she hurried me to her grave site where the flames had reached, crumbling the rock and fracturing the fragile strands of the willow.

"No. Anna, please." I begged for her to stay, my hands cradling her ethereal face. Though I offered her many opportunities to leave, telling her she did not have to linger, never did I think the day would come where she would.

Anna kissed my lips. A cold sensation yet so warm it touched my heart. She pulled away, smiled and mouthed "Love you", vanishing into nothingness.

Another cry of loss escaped me, my will to live slipping from my grasp.

With Holly gone and Anna sent to her final rest, the only thing keeping me focused lay in the desire to end Catalina.

She took my life, my lover and defiled my home. Scorching rage filled my soul.

"Evening, lover." The irritatingly seductive voice rose above the flames.

My shoulders drew up as I stood. "What have you done?"
Catalina asked me what I meant.

I repeated what I said, clenching my hands into fists at my sides.

"I did this all for you. Had you woken up and come to your senses, none of this would have been needed. I told you, Jonathan. This would never end until I bedded you. Until I possessed you."

There it is. "So, that is what this is for. I am nothing but something you cannot have." I turned on my heel to face her, my nails extended into the blades. My fangs grew, my eyes black with rings of silver. The true extent of my nature. "Then let us end this now."

Catalina cackled, her own nails extending. Instead of lunging at me, she sent her ghouls with a gesture of her head. "Careful my pets. I want him alive."

The alpha of the pack crept forward, challenging either of the ghouls standing at his flanks, daring them to break ranks and step in front of him.

They began forming a circle around me like wolves preparing to finish a wounded animal.

As the first one jumped, I leaned back as far as I could go to avoid its grasping fingers. It flew into its fellow ghoul, angering it.

The alpha lunged at my mid-drift, shoving me back until I slammed the sides of my hands down on his spine. Cracking of bone and a yowl of pain forced the ghoul to release me.

When he released me, I had mere moments to twist my body to avoid getting attacked by the second ghoul to receive a near blow to the face by the third.

Ghouls were the ideal slaves but in combat they could not maintain the level of intelligence needed to outthink a higher caste member of my kin.

On and on, I dodged, struck and parried until my body drew to the last of its adrenaline reserves. However, the ghouls also showed a level of fatigue.

In a last effort to follow their mistress' orders, they fell on me at once, pinning me down on my knees.

Snarling through my fangs, I tried to rise against them.

Laughing in apparent triumph, Catalina strolled towards us. "A noble effort but we both know, with the poison in your veins, you could not hold such stamina for long. Shall we give you another dose?"

In her hand, Catalina held the dagger she used in our earlier encounter. From the blade dripped a renewed application of the toxic substance. I readied myself for another thrust.

A shrill howl of agony from one of the ghouls alerted us all to the new arrival. The ghoul released me screaming in pain as the side of its skull began to melt like wax from a candle.

From its eye, protruded a bolt from a bow or crossbow. *A holy weapon.* I thought, amazed.

Another bolt and another struck the other two ghouls. Both released me to hollering in pain from bolts in their chest and cheek. They dropped to the ground, wriggling as the last vestiges of their lives faded from them.

Catalina turned, moving with enough time to avoid a direct hit to her. The tip of the arrow grazed her shoulder – enough to cause horrible pain.

If one has never experienced a holy weapon attack – especially a beast of the night – then you would not understand the absolute pain even a graze can cause.

Leland limped towards me, lugging the weapon, struggling to stand. "Bloody bitch. I've always hated tarts like you who believe they have a right to own a man."

"Why are you here? You will die," I asked, allowing Leland to help me stand.

Leland loaded another bolt. "You gave up your daughter, your home and your life for this blighter. It didn't feel right to let you fight alone. Besides, I still owe you a debt. Consider this payment."

There would be no arguing. Once a hunter made up their minds, nothing could change them.

Shrieking, Catalina flew from the shadows of her mist form, slashing across Leland's stomach deep enough to empty it. I remained frozen in horror, hating myself for not being more aware of her changing forms.

Leland choked on his blood, falling to his knee. One hand held his entrails while the other lifted the crossbow, firing but missing.

Catalina disappeared back into the night.

I took the opportunity to take Leland as far away as I could, setting him down against a tree.

It bewildered me to see he laughed through the blood. His words came out garbled. "Remember what I asked back at the shack?"

I nodded.

"Well, you better get to it. I don't think I'll last much longer."

Pain. A pain and fury at everything I endured became an inferno in my heart and mind. I held such respect for this man, loved my daughter, cared for Anna and even held a fondness for Walter.

Catalina took all of it away as she had centuries ago. I knew I would never see Holly again, I could never. Leland had remained hidden, living in the same city yet I never knew.

Walter nearly died protecting Holly and Anna gave me a life outside of the darkness, blood and murder until she was killed.

"She will pay for this," I said.

Leland smiled, coughing up more blood before saying "good."

Taking the hunter in my arms, I sank my fangs into his throat, drinking as one would from a bottle, the hunger so powerful I could not stop until I held his limp body. *I will lay you to rest soon. Sleep well, my friend and thank you.*

I lay Leland down on the soft Earth, stood with renewed strength and readied myself to return to the battle with Catalina.

XVIII. It All Ends in Flames...

The battlefield I beheld reminded me much of the first night the true evil of my story began. A jealousy, a delusion, a burning vineyard and a murder most wicked.

Instead of the scent of burning grapes, I tasted the scent of the flowers Holly cared so much for. I remembered when she danced amongst them, talking to the birds and singing.

Anna often joined Holly, keeping out of her line of sight, guarding Holly and loving her like a mother. It made me smile, those days of light where life gave me the audacity to hope.

Staring at the skeleton of Raven Hollow, I realized I lived a lie. A man's sins will catch up with him in time.

Chills ran up my spine from the demented presence behind me. With one last glance at the fountain in front of me, I whirled to see the melancholy eyes of Catalina Beauclair.

"Tell me why, Jonathan. I cared for you more than my own husband. I wanted him gone so we could be together. What did that mortal offer you that I could not?"

At my sides, my nails once again grew. My fangs, dripping with Leland's blood, glistened in the full moon light, full of vengeance and the rage of the bygone past. The gall she had to speak in such a way about Anna infuriated me.

Shifting into the black mist, I lunged towards Catalina, changing into a solid form and slashing at her, meeting her own blades.

She shifted into red mist, flying around me, changing and attacking in small increments.

With both of us at full capacity for strength, the fight could last days. The option I took teetered on the edge of a madman plagued by desperation.

I sprinted into the burning house, dodging the flames. Catalina followed, standing at the opposite end of the upstairs hallway.

Raising her nails, Catalina scratched the crumbling wallpaper, making her way towards me. "Brings back memories, does it not, beloved?"

I scoffed, my brows creased. Within the flames, I held the advantage. Here I had allies ready to aid me out of revenge for having their home destroyed.

Catalina chuckled, her fangs bared. It did not take long for the first spirit to lunge at her with such force it knocked her aside, making her curse.

I smiled at her frustration as spirit after spirit struck her. "It is not only my life you ruined. There are ghosts here who lived with me, respected and honored me. You angered them by burning down their home."

Catalina swung her nails at the unseen assailants, screaming and cursing as loud as she could.

I took one of the brittle fallen beams and slammed it down, sending Catalina through the floor into the basement.

Through the flames, I looked down to see her body pinned beneath the weight of the rafters and support beams.

Spirits looked up at me, some crying, others nodding to let me know they would hold her there until the house crumbled completely.

Thanking them, I changed into the form of the Great Dane, running through the falling structure until I arrived outside.

Thank you, my friends. May you rest in peace. I sat in the falling snow, howling a mournful howl as the last of my home crumbled.

The arrival of the police and local fire control told me I needed to leave in haste. I hid as a raven amidst the shadows listening to them.

Abrams stood with the same officers, eyes bulging, mouths agape. "What the bloody hell happened here?" Abrams asked.

"It's a mystery. I was unaware anyone even lived here except that witch girl who liked the company of the dead," his older companion said.

The reference made me angry. I flew off into the night, catching a glimpse at Abrams who looked in my direction with a puzzled look on his face.

* * *

I returned to the place I left Leland's body, taking off the ash covered duster and draping it over him prior to raising him in my arms. *Hold on, my friend. I will take you to a place worthy of such a noble man.*

In spite of the night's events, the calls of the owls and hunting foxes brought a smile to my face. Hushing whispers of the snow calmed my burning soul with its cool touch on my cheeks.

Here. I set Leland down against the thick root of an old oak I spent a great deal of time with. The old tree appeared to listen to me during the days before Holly arrived in my life. Digging at the snow, into the loose earth, I prepared a proper grave.

Somehow I knew the hunter would want me to take the crossbow but I chose to bury it with him. *A warrior should be laid to rest with his weapon. I hope you can forgive me if this is not what you wanted.*

Once the earth took possession of Leland's body, I took a flat stone, using my nails to chisel his name so history would never forget him.

Until dawn, I held a silent vigil over the hunter's grave then departed on whatever path life held for me.

XIX. And So it Begins...Again

London, Modern Day

Around early evening, the pub filled with patrons eager to drink away a long day of work. Exhaust from cars permeated the streets, replacing the carriages I knew. How I missed the sound of horses and creaking wheels on cobblestone. Horns replaced the shouts of agitated cabbies trying to get the public to move out of their way so they could reach their destination.

The glass cup in my hand felt so foreign to me as I cleaned it with a black towel. Out of the corner of my eye, I could see a young woman talking with her friends, their giggles a sign as to what would happen.

In light of the events at Raven Hollow, I decided not to risk the lives of anyone else.

My attention drew to two gentlemen speaking at the far end of the bar.

"Did you hear? Someone's rebuilding the old Raven Manor." The skinnier of the two with dark brown hair commented to his chubby friend.

"Really? After what happened? Who would do such a thing?" The chubby man asked.

I could not help but smile. It had been a decision I made –
to turn my old home into a museum dedicated to the spirits who
aided in my escape from the fire.

In truth, it held the same reason why I stayed as long as I did
in the olden days. No one found the entrance to the crypt holding
the coffin chained with silver.

I never left London, knowing once I did, someone would
happen upon it and release the demon within. No longer did I
reside there but remained protective.

"I heard the man is a private connoisseur of older houses.
Retains history or something like that," the skinny man said.

Is that what they say? I laughed.

One of the young ladies came up to the bar, a bright blush
on her face. I recognized her as a regular patron. "Evening John. I
was wondering -"

"Forgive me, but I cannot give you what you seek." I cut her
off, watching her walk away, saddened that I had to hurt her.

Through the doors, walked a woman resembling someone
dear to me. My eyes widened in shock.

Anna? It could not be her but she did have a sister who
looked remarkably the same. Had Anna not told me how old she
was, I would have thought them twins.

The woman walked up to the counter, setting her purse on
the bar.

I joined her, asking her what brought her in that evening. "It
appears I'm a bit lost. I'm supposed to meet with a friend but do not
know where Central Park is. I know it's late but she wanted me to
see the lights of the autumn festival."

She stared, her eyes analyzing me. "I'm sorry, but, do I
know you? Your eyes seem familiar," The woman turned away
laughing. "I know it's silly. May I ask for a cup of water please?"

It did not sound silly to me. Even if she never knew me,
blood held a strong bond between family members. I handed her a
glass of water, giving her directions and asking her if she might want
someone to accompany her.

Blushing, she assured me I did not have to. As an English
gentleman, I told her I did not mind. "Then, my name is Hannah.
Hannah Billingsly."

Following my shift at the bar, I left with her. Somehow, the walk ended at her loft where she apologized profusely, saying she never did anything like this before.

I brushed my fingers over her cheeks, laden with guilt at how my charm managed to do as it had to so many others. I knew without a fragment of doubt, this woman was related to Annabelle. Her blood, her eyes, even the manner in which she carried herself all betrayed her family lineage.

"There is no need to apologize." I kissed her forehead, recognizing her scent. "Hannah, by any chance are you related to someone named Annabelle Price?"

The question appeared to take her aback. "She was my great great Aunt, or something like that. How do you know her?"

I left the question unanswered, kissing Hannah's lips, fighting the pain in my heart. My fangs longed to taste her blood but I fought them. Never had I drank from Anna or taken any sexual energy from her. I would not do it to her niece.

At the end of the night, despite what my body wanted, I left the loft, allowing Hannah to live in a dream. She would not remember me but she would have the instructions for how to get to Central Park.

* * *

Tired from the encounter with Hannah, I returned to my own loft. One of the tenants an older woman named Ms. Nibbitz stopped me in the hallway.

"John! I have something for you."

I turned to see the old woman scuttling down the hallway in her slippers, her hair up in curlers.

Behind her, one of her cats skittered, mewling at her. In her hand, she held what looked like a letter and a rose.

Ms. Nibbitz stopped before me, breathing heavily from the exertion. "A lovely young woman brought these for you. Asked me to give them to you and only you."

My heart palpitated at recognizing the white rose with red tips on its petals. I thanked Ms. Nibbitz and went into my loft, refusing to open the letter and setting the rose on top of it.

From an old trunk beneath my bed, I pulled old portraits of Holly and Anna.

I attended Holly's funeral where Walter recognized me yet did not point me out in respect to my silent shake of the head. He did not look like himself but a gentleman who experienced the effects of time.

A year later, I attended his funeral, meeting a little girl who called me beautiful and held out an orchid which I pressed for longevity.

I set the portraits aside. *There is no use in denying the inevitable.* I thought, taking the letter, opening it despite already knowing who sent it.

Dearest,
I have found you at last. Did you think you escaped me?
I know of your new name. It is a shameful replacement to the power
and influence your old name held.
This will never be over until one of us dies.
I remain your lover and pray we meet soon.

~ Catalina

My heart sank at the final words yet I knew she spoke the truth. What evil lurked beneath the fog of London would never end until one of us breathed our last...

Enjoy this exclusive sneak peek available only in the paperback copy! Aren't you a lucky one!!

Hell's Warden
Coming 2020

1.

Can one ever truly understand the nature of Hell? Are religion, science or philosophy the only glimpses man has ever taken into the raging inferno? I can tell you now, I have seen Hell.

Its face consisted of nightmares no mortal mind could ever perceive. Monsters capable of rending flesh from bone poured from Hell's maw during the first event known as the Scourge. Its memory forever haunts me, for it served as a reminder of how easily alliances can crumble when humanity needs a sacrifice.

I pushed away the thoughts of the past, returning to the feeling of the demon writhing beneath the sole of my boot. Its poison-laced tongue lashed about, attempting to meet whatever manner of flesh it could find. Claws thicker than the teeth of the Mosasaurs of old, gripped and tore at the Venetian cobblestone streets in an attempt to break free.

Hissing curses damning me to Hell flowed from its throat resulting in acidic saliva dripping to the ground, burning it.

Tired of its chatter, I loaded Charon, the tri-barreled gun blade, and pressed it into the side of the demon's jaw. With a mighty roar, the sacred bullets dispatched the beast screeching and howling in pain back from whence it came.

No matter how many of these damn bastards I kill, it always seems like ten more take its place. Holstering Charon beneath the pitch black duster, I lowered the brimmed hat over my face, turning my attention to the alternate reason I had been sent out that cold, rainy evening.

In front of me, a cracking tear, flashing with lightning and reeking of the stench of rotten corpses and Sulphur snaked and curled. From my belt, I took what would look to an onlooker to be nothing more than a hand-grenade with a red cross painted messily on the side of it. I removed the pin with my teeth and casually tossed it into the Fissure. It exploded, causing the scar to shatter into pieces of glass before falling to the earth.

A satisfied grin curled across my lips.

My name is Markus Slayde, and I am known as Hell's Warden.

**

"Sent you out again, I see." I looked up from the bar to stare into the eyes of one of the most beautiful women in creation. Long, silken strands as black as night drifted over milky skin in luscious waves. Eyes burning the gold of a dragon's glare appeared to glow beneath layers of nightshade make-up. To men, she would be a treasure with her hourglass figure and flawlessly voluptuous breasts.

Unfortunately for her, I knew her true nature.

I said nothing at first, choosing to meet her lusting stare with my own blazing orange, then answering. "It would seem so."

The woman slid closer, leaning over the bar, her nails stroking the knuckles holding the glass long empty of beer. She chuckled through closed lips, made a kissing gesture and took the glass to go refill it, returning.

In a teasing voice, she resumed tracing my knuckles. "Now, now, Warden. Is that anyway to treat an old friend?"

I scoffed at her. Dagon, a succubus, a temptress of men, never became regarded as a friend. In a distant past, she remained one of the many prisoners I kept in check during the Scourge - an enemy the Church ordered me to kill on sight should she ever escape Hell. Her use of my title – or previous title – enraged me to the point I wanted to kill her. However, in her recent years, Dagon proved a valuable source of information during my nightly hunts.

As if she knew the thoughts in my mind, Dagon toned down her flirting, backing off and proceeding to fiddle with a glass and a towel. "In any case, Hell is in an uproar over your return. We long thought you dead and out of our way."

It didn't surprise me. Following my imprisonment, I heard rumor that Hell did all but dance in a full-fledged rave. A celebration so strong the Earth experienced it in many demonic forms – many too satanic to mention.

Dagon continued speaking but I ignored her, drinking my fill of the swill her bar tried to call Venetian Scotch. After a while, she left me to my own devices, aware of each of the burning, hate-filled eyes of the patrons.

One of them, a large man who up until now, sat in the far corner of the bar in a semi-circle shaped booth, walked up behind me with two of his men. I recognized the putrid smell of Sulphur mixing with rancid sweat and body odor. *Great, possessed. My favorite.*

The man spoke in a foreign accent older and more evil than Italian, a low hiss beneath his baritone voice. All around me, onlookers stopped, ready for the spectacle unfolding before them.

When I refused to address the demon, it gripped my shoulder in a firm vice, spinning me in the chair and leaning into my face. The nauseating body odor met with cigarette smoke, gasoline and old liquor. To avoid retching, I had to turn away.

Angry, the demon addressed me again in the same demonic language, demanding me to leave the bar so we could fight.

Taking another drink from my Scotch, I pushed the man's hand off. "Sorry Tiny, you and your friends will have to find another partner to dance with. I'm done here."

The next thing I knew, patrons started screaming as all Hell broke loose. All three men began writhing and contorting like they experienced a severe seizure. Limbs elongated, teeth grew into those of a shark, and eyes once natural colors turned into beads of black with blazing red irises.

Classical signs of possession. I stood from the stool, casually taking Charon from its holster and loading it. "You boys really should've seen someone before it got this bad. Guess I'll have to be your exorcist."

The alpha demon lunged at me first, arms and hands reaching out to grab a hold of me. I bent backwards to avoid him, hitting him in the back of the head with Charon's grip. Dazed, the demon flew forward into the bar. Behind it, Dagon smirked, watching the carnage.

Another demon, a gangly man with a bald head covered with a blue bandana wrapped his arms around my shoulders from behind while his friend proceeded to punch me in the stomach. *Typical. Can't fight on their own so they gang up on you.*

Using the strength of the man behind me, I raised my legs and kicked out at the one in front. It sent him stumbling backwards while Gangly held me taut to his body. Throwing my head back, I nailed Gangly in the face hard enough to make him scream.

The large man, whom I dubbed Tiny, threw his weight into me from the back, sending us both through the glass window of the bar into the street.

High- pitched ringing in my ears made rising from the ground slower than I intended until Tiny hauled me to my feet and proceeded to hit me.

With one hard punch, Tiny sent me flying over the hood of a parked car. A woman screamed, making the throbbing headache I'd begun developing ache even worse.

In all the confusion, I'd lost Charon. Without it, the fight wouldn't only be difficult, it'd be impossible for me to exorcise the demon.

"Dammit." I grunted, standing, eyes scanning the ground for Charon. I found it lying near the curb behind an angry demon. "Fuck."

Tiny attempted to lunge at me again only to be stopped abruptly when a silver blade thrust its way through his chest. Bone splinters and blood spurted, splashing me in the face and covering my duster. Tiny threw his arms out in the manner of someone being crucified, his chest burst forward.

A horrifying scream followed briefly before the body crumpled to the cold, wet ground.

Behind him, a man in a black business suit stood holding a blade at his side. His golden hair and light eyes betrayed him as being someone I'd rather shoot myself than see.

He walked over to me, offering a handkerchief. "A good evening to you, Warden. I fear you and I must talk."

About the Author

Iona Caldwell is a lover of all things arcane. An avid reader, Iona has had a love of books for as long as she's been able to read. She is a very active book reviewer, capable of reading up to four books in a single month (paperbacks are preferred, thank you very much). As an active and outspoken druid, Iona loves to spend time in her garden. She enjoys hiking, foraging and sitting in the moon when it's full. She is currently working on her second novel, *Hell's Warden* due to be released next year. As an author, Iona pledges never to write a series, claiming she wants her readers to be able to enjoy a story for what it is. She currently lives in Texas with her two children, husband, a dog and a cat.

www.ionacaldwell.weebly.com
www.theantleredcrown.weebly.com

Acknowledgments

I want to thank so many people who have made this book a possibility. My husband and kids have been one of the most supportive groups of people I have. When I started this journey, I had no idea what to expect and have come to meet some amazing authors and bloggers along the way. I thank my Instagram community, primarily Mike Salt, who has been so kind and reassuring in times of doubt.

I want to thank my publisher for doing all they've done so far. When I met the FyreSyde team in person, I never thought a small press would be willing to do as much to help me build my platform. I'd heard so many horror stories about traditional publishers.

My editors are amazing people. They are very fast and gave me some amazing feedback to help *Beneath London's Fog* become the story that it is.

I want to thank my beta readers who offered their time to offer feedback and the bookbloggers who have offered their time to review my book.

And of course, I want to thank my readers. All of you are such a great team of people who help make the writing community what it is. I can't wait to bring you all my titles and see what you think about them.

I want to thank the inspirations in the literary world – Stephen King, Neil Gaiman, Darcy Coates, Nick Cutter, Guillermo del Toro, and Clive Barker – who continue giving us tales of magic, terror and wander.

I can't wait to grow in this journey with all of you!!

Thanks for reading our Beneath London's Fog! Please add a short review on Amazon, Goodreads, your blogs, etc and let me know what you thought!

Here you hold the paperback in your hands! We hope you enjoyed the secret peek into *Hell's Warden,* Iona's next book (something the ebooks don't have). FyreSyde wants to offer our authors' readers a chance to get exclusive sneak peeks into our upcoming titles. Subscribe to our newsletter and like us on Facebook to be added to a secret group on Facebook! Members receive monthly looks at giveaways, sales pricing, chapter blurbs, upcoming titles, cover reveals, and trailers months in advance. Subscribe to Iona's page for short stories around her novellas and much more!!